I0553943

Lilacs, Litigation, and Lethal Love Affairs

by

J L Wilson

Lilacs, Litigation, and Lethal Love Affairs

Cover Art by *Kim Mendoza*

The Wild Rose Press
PO Box 708
Adams Basin, NY 14410-0706
Visit us at www.thewildrosepress.com

Publishing History
First Crimson Rose Edition, 2011
Print ISBN 1-60154-900-8

Published in the United States of America

He glanced at me.
"Most women would say it's just a plant."

I snorted. "And a rose is just a rose. We know better." Our eyes met and for an instant I felt as though we were in perfect harmony with each other, looking deeply into our individual souls. Then Houdi tapped the pages in Sam's hands and the moment vanished. "I really didn't hear much more. I did hear something about stock options. You were demanding to be given options in his company, right?"

Sam nodded. "It seems only fair. After all, it was my work that helped create some of the products his company is producing." He frowned down at the inventory information he held. "We can use the money. I'd like to invest it back in the business." Then he looked up at me guiltily, as though suddenly aware he shared personal information with a total stranger.

"That makes sense to me," I agreed, standing up carefully so I didn't tread on Houdi or Sam, both watching me with similar alert, hopeful looks. "I can stop by the office tomorrow and talk about it if you like," I volunteered, gesturing to the papers he held.

Sam stared at me for a second or two longer then stood. "I'd appreciate it if you could. I think this will be useful and if we can implement it as soon as possible, I want to do it."

My mail icon pinged and I leaned over, clicking open the mailbox. *You deserve not to be ignored by women.* "It sounds like a fortune cookie," I said with a laugh.

He grinned, the little fans around his eyes deepening. "Well, as long as the right woman pays attention, I guess it doesn't matter." He stared down at me, his eyes suddenly dark and mysterious. "Right?"

I may have been out of practice with men, but even I could see the invitation in his dark eyes.

Dedication

To the Landscape Horticulture instructors at DCTC, who made my fifth foray into higher education fun as well as practical. I will never view nursery operations the same way again.

Chapter 1

The angry voices were getting louder.

I crouched behind the double-shelved potting bench full of glossy green philodendrons and tried to peer through the leaves at the argument in progress on the far side of the greenhouse. Two men had come into the house while I was bent over to straighten the plastic pots on the floor and they obviously didn't know I was there. Heck, even if I were standing straight they might not see me among the verdant vegetation that surrounded me. I was short and the greenery was tall and thick.

"You've sold out, Mike, and you know it," one man said, his voice deep, low and angry. "I can't believe you took everything we worked for and threw it away like that. You son of a bitch, I should expose you. You deserve it." I couldn't see the speaker because he was standing next to the palm bench and was hidden by the fronds but he sounded royally pissed off.

"Threw it away? Who are you kidding? I'm making a six-figure salary and I'm on the board of Min-Gen Technologies. I'll retire in a couple of years on my stock options. Where are you? Still peddling

1

petunias? Still crawling around in the dirt and doing landscape designs? How's the company doing? Will you show a profit this year?"

This came from the tall man in a business suit who stood in the aisle leading through the greenhouse past the dozens of wooden tables holding houseplants. I recognized him as the keynote speaker for today's dedication ceremony of the new greenhouse, which was situated next to this one where I now toiled. Dr. Michael Peavey was a research botanist who donated a large chunk of money to build the tech school's horticulture program here in Roseville, a suburb of Minneapolis. I'd endured his speech just an hour earlier but slipped away from the celebratory banquet to finish my chores in the old greenhouse.

"It's not about the money," the first man hidden in the palms said.

"Of course it is. You're lying if you say it isn't. I got the business and the patents and..." His voice was muffled as he turned then I heard him say, "...hated me all these years because of it. Don't blame me now because I'm a success. Your threats won't stop me."

"Threats? You haven't seen threats yet. Just wait until I tell—"

Their voices were drowned out by the creaking of the overhead fans kicking on in an attempt to keep the temperature regulated in the leaky old structure. I used the noise to duck low and scurry out of the side door leading to the hall in front of the horticulture classrooms.

"Hey, Gidget!"

I stopped and waited for the teenager to catch up to me as he hurried down the concrete block hallway. My younger classmates bestowed that nickname on me when one of them watched a Sixties TV marathon on cable TV and noticed my resemblance to the star of the television show of the same name. Sally Fields was ten years older than me, but we still looked remarkably alike although my short, shaggy hair had always been white. It was an odd quirk of aging that now as I approached fifty my hair was turning pale sweatshirt gray. Thank goodness the kids didn't latch onto the Flying Nun. That would have been too much, even for my easy-going nature.

"What's up, Aaron?" I asked, taking a left turn and approaching the main entry door to the greenhouse I'd just vacated. I glanced at the steamy glass door and saw a dark silhouette against its surface.

"They're getting ready to cut the ribbon on the new greenhouse. You have to make the speech, don't you? Ed sent me to find you."

"I'm on my way. I was just finishing up in the old greenhouse."

"It'll be nice working in the new house, won't it?" Aaron Swenson fell into step with me. He was one of the handsomest young men I've ever seen with a tall, athletic build, blond hair, and a sunny smile and disposition to match. His dark blue eyes always seemed to be mischievous and warm, as though every person he talked to was the center of his universe. He was charming, sweet, and sincere, or at least he seemed to be. Some people seemed that way until you really got to know them, but I suspected he truly was as nice as he seemed. No one could cultivate such a persona without slipping at least once in a while.

"I won't get much time in the new greenhouse," I commented. "I graduate in a few weeks and am off to the real world, such as it is."

Aaron looked surprised then nodded. "I keep forgetting you're ahead of us."

"Only relatively speaking," I assured him. "I

transferred in so many credits from my other schools it put me a year ahead of you guys." We walked down the hallway, nearing the main door to the greenhouse. As we did, the steamy glass door opened and a man burst out. The collar on his black leather jacket was pulled high, hiding most of his face so all I saw was his tousled white and gray hair. He brushed by us down the hall which led to the front entrance of the school building.

"Who's that?" Aaron asked as he peered back over his shoulder. He opened the door and I preceded him into the potting room that served as foyer to the newer greenhouse.

"No idea. I guess he's a visitor or something." I entered the twenty-foot open space, meagerly heated by the overhead pipes. Most of the Horticulture Department students were inside, mingling with a few school and town dignitaries who looked out of place next to the tubs of dirt, bags of fertilizers and plastic trays lining the wooden potting benches. Ed Jenkins, one of the instructors, gestured with his coffee mug for me to join him. I crossed the room to the big red ribbon stretched across the doorway to the new greenhouse.

"Cassie, this is Dr. Anderson, the school President." Ed beamed at me. "Dr. Anderson, this is Cassie Whittington. She's the president of the Student Horticulture Society. She'll be making the acceptance speech on behalf of our students."

I held out my hand, which was thankfully somewhat clean. "Nice to meet you."

Dr. Anderson was a tall, angular woman about twenty years my junior and svelter in her business-like blue pants and pretty silk blouse. Of course, I was transplanting tulips just an hour earlier, so my patched jeans and man's shirt over my T-shirt were more practical. I thought about my own business wardrobe, pushed to the back of my closet since the layoff three years earlier and wondered fleetingly if anything would still fit. I made a mental note to go through the clothing and donate a few items to charity. I doubted I'd be returning to the Business World any time soon.

"It's nice to meet you," she said. "Ed tells me you started working at Barlow's Nursery in Pickaway. That's a good company. We've placed a lot of students there over the years. Sam Barlow and Mary Hannon are real supporters of the program."

"I started there last month. It's convenient because it's so near my house. Aaron and I both started at the same time." I nodded toward Aaron, who had followed me into the room. "This is Aaron Swenson. He's the V.P. of the Horticulture club."

Dr. Anderson turned to Aaron and smiled. Everyone smiled when they saw Aaron. He reminded me a lot of my ex-husband, Charlie, who was also one of the handsomest men I've ever met. Charlie was unspoiled, rich, and likeable. If Aaron were lucky, he'd mature into a man like Charlie.

"Several of our grads have worked at Barlow's Pickaway store and at the Roseville store." Dr. Anderson looked past me at the clock high on the wall. "As soon as Dr. Peavey arrives, we'll get started."

"I saw him in the old greenhouse a few minutes ago," I said, jerking a thumb over one shoulder to the hallway. "He was talking with someone over by the big palms." Ed shot me an exasperated look and I added, "They were standing by the *Howea belmoreana*." I had struggled to memorize the Latin names in Ed's Interior Landscaping class and was gratified when he nodded. Apparently I got it right.

Dr. Anderson glanced at the clock again. I recognized impatience when I saw it. I edged toward the door. "I'll check and see if he's ready."

"I'll go." Aaron was already turning and

hurrying out of the potting room.

"Thank you." The prez turned to another student and I went to the new greenhouse, slipping under the big red ribbon and walking into the empty space. It was a beautiful structure, graceful and up-to-date with all the modern conveniences. Compared to the old house that leaked cold air in the wintertime and was stifling in the summer, this was like a little bit of heaven, a little bit of clean, fresh, and new heaven.

I joined the two members of the Elder Ladies League, or ELLs, a group of older women who had, like me, returned to school after layoffs or empty nest syndrome. "Ready for your ten minutes of fame?" Susan asked with a smile.

"I'm not talking for ten minutes, more like two."

"How's the new job going?"

"Pretty good. I think I'll like it. Of course, it's only about a mile from my house, so I love the commute." I spied food arranged on one of the wooden potting benches. My stomach rumbled at the sight. "It's so odd to be in a suburb after years of living downtown. Cows instead of cars."

"Have you met Sam Barlow yet?" Laurie Morrison asked.

"I heard he's sexy," Susan said. She was a petite, gray-haired woman whose husband retired young. They spent several weeks in Florida over the spring break and she still retained her tan, which emphasized her light gray eyes. "Joan Evenson said he was sexy. She works in the Roseville store and he manages it."

"I haven't met him yet. He's snowbirding in Florida. His sister Mary hired me. She runs the Pickaway store."

"He was a Marine," Laurie said. "I heard he served overseas then came back and went to college before going into business with his father. There's been a Barlow Nursery for almost a hundred years. I heard it's a good place to work. They pay well." She regarded me with alert curiosity.

I nodded. "I'm getting seven dollars over minimum."

"Man, that is good." Laurie was working at Landau's Nursery, the biggest garden center in the Twin Cities. They had five locations and Laurie worked at the Uptown center, where all the yuppies shopped. She always complained about the hours, which were long, and the clientele, which was snobby. "I'm only getting five over minimum."

"I think it was the computer stuff that did it." I eyed the cookies resting on a tray on one of the potting benches. In the last three years I shed seventy pounds and was now at my college weight of one-hundred-twenty. Surely one cookie wouldn't matter, would it? "I told Mary Hannon when I interviewed I could revamp their inventory system."

"Good bargaining chip." Susan looked envious and I knew it was because computers intimidated her. My twelve years in the high tech industry were proving to be handy in my post-layoff years.

"Can you?" Laurie asked. She was a slim blonde woman who, like me, had lost weight but unlike me, she didn't have to struggle to keep it off. Either that or she was a good actress and it only appeared that it was effortless. It might have been the latter because I could never quite tell what Laurie was thinking.

"Can I what?" I edged toward the cookies and the coffee urn nearby.

"Can you set up their inventory system?" She perched one butt cheek on a bench and leaned back slightly, letting a leg dangle back and forth. Her 'work' clothes—denim jeans and jacket over a dark T-shirt—still looked fresh and clean even after tussling with repotting plants in our propagation class earlier in the day. I always ended up looking like Pig Pen after a day at school but Laurie and Susan looked as if they just stepped out of the laundry room. Laurie regarded me skeptically. "I thought that sort of thing took months to implement."

"It does," I admitted. "But I've already tested the software. I did it for a project in my Nursery Management class. So I know how it works. Mary Hannon wants me to try it out on a subset of their operations this summer and if it looks good, we'll implement it completely in the fall, when they change stock for winter season."

"Sounds like you'll have a job for a while then," Susan said

I hadn't considered it, but she was right. Many nursery/landscape jobs were seasonal, but Mary didn't indicate it was short-term when she hired me. "We'll see," I said. "Inventory can be complicated to implement. We'll need to do new bar coding to get it to work."

"So you haven't met the boss yet?" Susan took a ginger cookie from the tray.

I took one, too, to keep her company. "Nope."

"I heard they're going to close the Pickaway center," Laurie commented, still swinging one leg casually.

"Really?" I nibbled the cookie, making the gingery goodness last as long as possible.

"I don't think it's a done deal," Susan said. Like me, she lived in Pickaway, a suburb to the west. She'd been a resident for decades, though, while I moved there just a few years earlier. "I know the county wants to widen the highway in front of their corner. Of course, they've been talking about doing that for years."

I visualized the scene in my mind. Barlow's Landscape Center was located on the corner of a busy county highway on the north and an equally busy boulevard on the east. A small lake bordered it on the west while townhomes, one of which was mine, encroached from the south. It was a prime piece of real estate in a fast-growing suburb. "I haven't heard anything about it," I said as I savored my cookie.

"Hey, Gidget," a voice hissed behind me.

I turned. Another student, Bobby Somebody, was gesturing to me from the doorway. "That must be my cue," I said, popping the last of the cookie in my mouth. I joined him near the big red ribbon. "Did Aaron find our main event?"

"I don't know. We can't find him anywhere. You said you saw Dr. Peavey in the greenhouse?"

"Yeah, just a few minutes ago. He was talking to a guy."

"He's not there now. What should we do?"

"Maybe he went to the administrative offices." I looked at my instructors, all standing with the college president. "Let's check."

I ducked under the red ribbon and headed for the door just as it opened and Aaron came in. He looked anxious and worried. "Did you find him?" I asked.

"What? Who? Oh, no. No, I went to the greenhouse but he wasn't there." Aaron looked past me to the college president, who was regarding us expectantly. "I looked everywhere."

I doubted it but I wasn't going to say it out loud. Aaron looked frazzled enough as it was without me criticizing his efforts. "Let's see what they want to do."

We joined the president and our instructors and had a huddled conference then Ed said, "Let's go ahead and do the ribbon cutting. Maybe Peavey was called away." He handed me a pair of the faux gold scissors and handed the other pair to Dr. Anderson.

"You two ladies can do the honors."

She and I stepped to the ribbon and the assembled students and visitors hushed. Ed introduced us then I gave my brief little *gee, this is great, it'll be neat for the students, we appreciate the matching funds you bigwigs donated* speech.

Dr. Anderson stepped forward and gave a brief, sincere speech and patted us all on the back, metaphorically speaking, for a fund-raising job well done. She and I turned to the ribbon and whacked it, the thick cloth falling aside to let the spectators move forward.

Polite applause greeted our efforts as the ribbon dropped to the concrete floor. The guests walked into the space, oohing and ahhing over the clean potting tables, bright sunlight streaming in, and the engraved paving stones donated during the fund-raising. I'd hit up the Whittington family for donations and several pavers were there with their names on them. I eyed John Whittington's paver and wished I could tread on it with my dirty, manure-covered work boots. John wasn't my favorite person.

About twenty minutes after the ceremony the crowd started to thin. The ELLs had long vanished, many to home and family and a few to jobs. Like me, many of them were working part-time while in school and all had commitments after the class day ended.

I picked up two of the Boston ferns we used as table decorations and started back through the potting room. "I'll put these back in the greenhouse," I told Ed as I passed him near the door.

"Thanks. I'll bring the other props in as soon as the crowd leaves."

I went to the old greenhouse and pushed open the door, drinking in the humid smells of dirt, plants and the sharp tang of fertilizer. The odors were a balm to my winter-weary senses. March in

Minnesota is a month of tantalizing hope and we still had half-a-foot of snow on the ground. This greenhouse was an oasis in the desert.

I walked along the narrow entry aisle, paved with flat stones that lay unevenly on the gravel floor. This walkway led into the greenhouse proper, the three-tiered tables on either side loaded with ficus, spider plants, dumb canes, bromeliads and ivy. The plants effectively blocked my view of all but the intersection ahead and the bright afternoon sunlight over me.

I reached the intersection for the main aisle and looked to my right. Four three-tiered benches lined either side of the aisle, each loaded with assorted plants. The Boston ferns were kept in the center of the greenhouse, where the humidity was less variable in the leaky structure. I turned to walk to my left, into the main part of the greenhouse and as I did, I almost fell over a body.

Michael Peavey was stretched out on the floor, overturned plants, dirt, and pots scattered over and around him. My first thought was that he'd fallen. Then I got a closer look at his face. I've never seen anyone with cyanosis before, but I recognized the symptoms. They were drilled into those of us who took Nursery Operations 101. Michael Peavey had all the signs of a man with pesticide poisoning—fixed and rigid limbs, a blue tinge to his face, bulging eyes, and protruding tongue.

I froze for one long, awful second. Then I realized whatever poisoned him could still be in the air if it had been released as a vapor. I turned to flee and that's when I saw the thin trail of blood, bright red against the white of a broken ceramic pot on the floor. I hesitated—was he just injured or was he dead?

I hazarded another look at his face and what I saw convinced me to get the hell out while I could. I dropped the ferns in a crashing explosion of busted pots and dirt then dashed out of the greenhouse, almost overturning a bromeliad on the way. I burst into the hallway then into the potting room, barreling into Ed Jenkins, who chatted with a group of students near the door. I grabbed his arm, almost spilling his ever-present coffee cup from his hand.

He took one look at my panicked face and set the mug down on a nearby table. "Is there a problem?"

An important dignitary and the chief donor to the school dead of pesticide poisoning in the Horticulture Department greenhouse? A problem?

That was the understatement of the year.

Chapter 2

Three hours later I was finally allowed to go home. The HazMat team, medical examiner, police, newspaper reporters and TV reporters all came and went during that time. At first Dr. Anderson insisted on calling Peavey's death an 'unfortunate accident' until I pointed out that her wording implied someone at the school was negligent. I'm sure visions of a lawsuit danced in her head because she declined comment after that and told the reporters she would issue a statement when the police had a chance to 'pursue further investigations.'

I explained two or three times, to two or three different detectives, how I overheard Peavey and the unknown man talking and also detailed the little I could remember of their conversation. Once the HazMat team determined there were no toxins in the air, I took the police into the greenhouse to show them where I stood, where the men stood, and the route I took into and out of the greenhouse. I saw the police talking to Aaron, his face white and pinched. He kept shaking his head, looking insistent. I suppose they were pressing him about where he had searched earlier. The poor kid looked scared to death.

Now Ed walked out with me to the parking lot, a pile of papers tucked under one arm and his travel mug of coffee in his free hand. "At least we can prove it wasn't our pesticides that killed him," he commented as we approached the parking lot now filling with students attending evening classes. "Everything was locked up and accounted for."

I knew this was a source of relief to him and the other instructors. They were ultimately responsible for the safety of the students and the school where the pesticides and insecticides were concerned. The HazMat team found no residue of pesticide in the air and the medical examiner had been close-lipped about possible causes of death. "It had to be inhaled," I said as we paused by Old Faithful, my ancient green Jeep Wrangler.

"Why do you say that?" Ed sipped his coffee as he watched me stow my gym bag full of dirty school clothes in the back of the Jeep alongside my book bag.

"He was alive just a few minutes before. In order for him to die so quickly he had to either swallow or inhale something. He was a trained chemist and botanist. There's no way he'd swallow anything left sitting around in a greenhouse." I wrinkled my nose at the thought. "It worked so fast it had to be inhaled."

"Well, I'm glad you're okay. I meant to ask you earlier, but forgot about it in the excitement...how's your job going at Barlow's?" Ed started to amble toward the staff parking lot, visible through the trees that separated the student lot from staff.

"Fine so far. I appreciate the recommendation you gave me. I'm sure it helped convince them I could do the job." I slid behind the steering wheel, settling my Happy Bunny pillow behind my back. "I think Mary Barlow was worried if a woman my age could keep up with the kids."

Ed grinned. He and I were about the same age, so I'm sure he knew what I meant. Nursery operation was really a job for the young, not for us middle-aged folks, unless you counted management, where age was often a benefit. A large part of my day was occupied with physical labor and I had the aching muscles to prove it.

"I'll lay you odds Mary is counting on you keeping the kids in line. I'm sure you'll do fine." He started to walk away then paused. "Did they catch the guy who was attacking women?"

I shook my head. The Pickaway Pervert had terrorized our town for the last three weeks. Two women were attacked in their homes. The police had no clues how the intruder entered because there was no sign of a break-in. The last attack came four days ago when a woman left her home to walk her dog at dusk. The attacker was lying in wait for her when she came back and was scared away when she screamed and two joggers who happened to be nearby came to the house to check on the noise. "Nope, he's still on the prowl."

"Be careful. That nursery area is dark in the morning. You might want to ask Mary if another employee can handle the early morning watering."

"Yeah, I might." I slammed my door, not telling Ed I didn't want to rock the boat in my new job. My ability to get to the nursery grounds early in the morning was a key factor for me being hired and I wasn't going to let my worries about a potential attacker screw up a good job. I would just be extra vigilant when I was at the nursery alone.

I drove twelve miles to the west to Pickaway, where I had settled after being laid off from my upper management job in Minneapolis three years ago. The place still had a small town feel despite the encroaching suburbs popping up on the northern fringes. I had just moved into my townhouse from my previous apartment a few weeks earlier. Between school and work, I still wasn't unpacked.

I fed Houdini, my fat yellow cat then plopped down on the couch with a beer and a bag of microwave popcorn. Peavey's death led the news. I was pleased to see there was no suggestion the Horticulture department was to blame. I kept one ear tuned to the news as I unpacked three more boxes, my daily goal.

By nine o'clock I was showered and snuggled in bed with Houdi curled up on my feet, my class notes spread out on the bed next to me as I studied for my upcoming finals. The Horticulture students had a truncated winter semester because spring was our busy time and most of us had jobs either in progress or waiting for us. So our study load was accelerated, allowing us to finish classes by early April. I was in my last semester of school and when I finished, I would have an A.A.S. degree in Landscape Horticulture to add to my B.S. and M.S. in Computer Science. Between my salary at Barlow's Nursery and my investments, I was facing a relatively comfortable semi-retirement.

The phone rang. I leaned over to check Caller ID. "Hey, Charlie," I said as I picked up the portable phone.

"I heard about a guy keeling over today at the school. What happened?"

I lay back in my blankets and nudged Houdi with my foot. He grumbled before rolling over to give my legs some breathing room. "I'm not sure. I saw the guy just minutes before he died."

"You saw him? Where?"

I heard the concern in his voice. Charlie and I grew up together and were married a brief seven years. We stayed friends since our divorce decades earlier and I was still considered a part of the

Whittington family, which I considered a mixed blessing at best.

I described how I was lurking in the greenhouse and the argument I heard. "Sounds like you might have almost witnessed the murder," Charlie commented.

"Might have almost," I laughed. "I'm not too worried. The police didn't appear interested in me."

"That's a relief. Are we still on for Saturday?"

"I think so."

"What do you mean, 'I think so'?" Charlie's voice was exasperated. "You promised, Cassie. We all have to sing, remember? You promised you'd sing solo, too. Besides, there's no way in hell I'm going to Grandy Theo's funeral without you there to protect me."

I tapped the screen of my Palm Pilot, confirming what I knew. "Yep, we're good. I got the day off. I need to study in the morning."

"I can't wait to see John's face when the lawyers read the will." Charlie's younger brother John always disliked me and the feeling was mutual. Charlie cherished those times when he could put John's boxers in a bunch.

"I still say you must be wrong." I yawned. "I loved your grandmother and I loved having tea with her all these years, but I doubt she left me anything in her will."

"Grandy adored you, especially after you told my father off."

I smiled at the memory. Charlie's father was a dictatorial tyrant who terrorized his wives and four children. At one family Christmas his father criticized Charlie's stepmother for having ham instead of turkey on Christmas Eve. I told his father to get his ass into the kitchen to cook if he thought he could do so much better. "That was the last Christmas party I ever attended with your family."

"The old man's mellowed the last few years," Charlie said. "I think you'd be surprised. Thanks for going with me, Cassie. You're a real friend."

I didn't believe his father could change, but I wouldn't quibble. "Well, you know what they say. Friends help you move. Real friends help you move the body."

Charlie laughed. "I'll keep it in mind."

"I'm glad we're doing the service on the first Saturday of the month. Grandy and I always had tea on the first Saturday afternoon. I can keep the tradition going." I tossed my Palm back on the books. "There's also something eerily appropriate about getting together with your family on April Fool's Day."

"No kidding."

"How're things going with you and Kathleen?"

There was a long pause. "We broke up."

"Charlie! She was nice."

"She was too possessive."

"You and she have been dating for almost a year. Maybe she had...expectations."

"Not from me, she didn't," he muttered. "I don't know. It got a bit confining. I guess I'm just not the settling-down kind." There was a pause then he said, "The longest I ever stuck with anybody was when I was married to you."

"And look how that turned out," I said, eyeing my pile of textbooks. "Don't worry, Charlie. The right girl is out there for you."

"Maybe." He sounded doubtful. "How's the security at your new townhouse? Did they get the alarm system installed?"

I thought guiltily of the security keypad which I neglected to activate when I came home. I wasn't accustomed to high tech gadgets looking out for my safety. "Yep, it's up and running."

"Good. I heard those news stories about the

mugger. You keep an eye out and stay safe."

The concern in his voice was heartening. "I will, Charlie." I looked with regret at the stack of papers scattered around my bed. "I've got to study. I'll see you on Saturday."

"Okay. And Cassie?"

"Hmm?"

"Set the alarm."

I sighed. "You know me too well, Charlie."

"Forty-five years of acquaintance does that. Good night."

"Night." I hopped out of bed, traversing the living room then crossing the kitchen to the door leading to the garage. I read the instructions for the tenth time then hesitantly touched the numbers to set the alarm. Satisfied I was relatively safe for the night, I went back to bed and my fourteen-pound feline companion. I fell asleep with my pesticide manual on my stomach, which probably contributed to the nightmares I endured, dreaming of Michael Peavey chasing me in the greenhouse.

I got up at five the next morning and by six I was wrestling with the metal gate separating Barlow's Landscape Center from the boulevard on the eastern edge of the landscape property. The gate was fifteen feet long and almost six feet high. Since I'm five-three and weigh around one-hundred-twenty pounds, the heavy metal gate often won the match by swinging shut to catch me by surprise.

It didn't help that today I was fumble-fingered with fear and my hands were freezing. I had spotted a pickup truck as I pulled up to the gate, sitting there with its lights off while the motor ran. The center wouldn't open until eight, so it couldn't be a customer and it wasn't daylight for another hour. Maybe it was just a person talking on a cell phone or looking at a map.

Or maybe it was something else. I didn't want to

wait around and find out. I slipped off my canvas gloves to punch in the combo code on the padlock and the March frost on the metal soaked into my fingers.

Few cars were on the road, making the idling pickup truck on the street obvious, even more so because the dark color was silhouetted against snow piled high against the curb. It was far enough away that the occupant was hidden in the shadow from the streetlight. I could easily imagine a husky man inside, a man who looked very like the police sketch artist's rendition of the creep who'd been preying on women for the last two weeks in our little corner of Minnesota. I punched in the combination again on the padlock and it sprang apart with a satisfying snick, loud in the frigid air.

I manhandled the gate open then scrambled into my ancient Jeep, grinding the gears in my haste to get into the relative safety of the parking lot surrounding the landscape center. I drove past the gate, hopped out, and clanged the gate shut behind me all in a matter of seconds. As I did, I saw the truck was no longer idling. The engine was shut off.

I had a sudden image of the headline in the *Pickaway Post*, the town newspaper: *Cassie Whittington, 50, found molested outside Barlow's Nursery. Police suspect she is the third victim of the Pickaway Pervert. Local authorities are investigating.* My imagination made me bolt for my Jeep in record time. I slammed the door behind me, almost cutting off my foot in my haste, and tromped on the gas. The Jeep lurched forward. Fifty feet ahead the drive turned sharply to the left, leading into the garden center. I made the turn, skirting the fenced-in tree area where evergreens and a few maples awaited new homes. To my right the tall stacks of bagged mulch, topsoil, and gravel hid my view of the county road in front of the lot on the north.

The security lights over the three greenhouses and the back storage yard lent more shadow than illumination. I drove behind the greenhouses to park then snatched my mini-bag out of my book bag before hurrying through the tree storage lot. Rows of burlap-wrapped trees hulked around me, all shipped from Barlow's production nursery in southern Minnesota.

I walked between the bulb greenhouse and the middle greenhouse, emerging at the back of the main building where the checkout counters, pottery, fertilizers, and other 'hard' stock were lined up, prepared for purchase by eager spring customers. The motion light came on as I approached the door. I already had my keys out and managed to get the heavy-duty metal door open on the first try, my breath flowing out in clouds of vapor.

"Springtime in Minnesota," I muttered in disgust as I pushed the door open. "I should move to Florida like the owners. They're in sun and fun while us peons struggle to open a stupid combination lock on their stupid gate for their stupid landscape business. Damn snowbirders. What a life."

The light switch was located on the wall, inside to the right. I flailed for it, as usual missing it on the first try and slamming my hand painfully against the metal bracket that held the switch. "Son of a bitch." I managed to find the button and the big main room flooded into well-lit life.

I hurried through the shelves of pre-emergent herbicides, bins of onion starter sets, racks of seeds, and displays of garden gloves. At the end of the forty-foot space I opened the door to the employee-only area and flicked on the overhead light. I got the coffee going then went to my locker and stowed my mini-purse and coat then dug out my work jacket and gloves. In a minute I was walking the length of the building, flicking on the overhead heaters. The noisy fans kicked on, bringing with them a thin thread of heat. I went to the door, prepared to go to the central greenhouse and start my daily chores.

As I slipped outside, I saw a light on the far side of the lot, in the back near the property edge. I hesitated, peering through the panes of the middle greenhouse, misted by the breaths of the pansies maturing inside. The light was definitely moving. Suburbs were encroaching on the landscape property and I often saw yard lights from the houses, partially shaded by tree branches moving with the wind.

Of course, if there were wind, I'd feel it here in the narrow walkway between the greenhouse in front of me and the main building behind me.

No wind.

I went back into the building, making a beeline for the phone near the coffee pot. I've read enough thrillers to know it's better to call the cops and have it be a false alarm than to end up the victim of a mugger. I dialed 911 with shaking hands. To my relief, I was answered promptly. "911, what's your emergency?"

"I'm at Barlow's Nursery, at the corner of County 42 and Barlow Boulevard. I think someone's on the grounds who shouldn't be here." I leaned against the counter and eyed the coffee. It smelled great.

"Cassie, is that you? Hold on, I'll check with Jake, he's on patrol tonight."

Charlene Hodgson was on duty. I visualized her plump, motherly face fringed by dark brown curls, peeking up over the high counter at the police station. She and Jolene Phelps took turns manning the front desk. I chatted with both of them a couple of weeks ago when I reported the vandalism at the greenhouse and also told them about the hang-up phone calls that plagued me occasionally when I opened the store early.

I wedged the phone receiver between my shoulder and ear as I snatched my *Of course I don't look busy, I did it right the first time* mug from the counter near the tiny sink. The phone cord let me stretch far enough to grab the sugar then the phone base began a precarious slide off the counter. I missed a couple of words as I maneuvered the receiver back to my ear.

"...right out, he's over by the Git 'n' Go gas station on Vernon. You hang tight. I don't know why Mary has you come in to open. They should have one of the boys out there. Didn't they hire a boy at the same time they hired you?"

I started to relax. Vernon Avenue was only two blocks away. A cop could be here in minutes. "Aaron lives on the other side of town and I live just a few blocks away. So it makes more sense for me to open. Thanks, Charlene. I wasn't sure if I should call it in or not. I get nervous sometimes out here alone." I poured my coffee, added the sugar, and sipped gratefully at the hot brew.

"I still say Mary Hannon should have a man out there."

"It's only for a few weeks. By Easter we'll have more staff out here early in the morning. For now they just need me and a couple of other kids to take care of things." I sipped again, leaning against the counter as I eyed the high ceiling where the fans were whirring, pushing warm air down to me. The concrete floor under my feet was still cold. I felt it even through the soles of my boots. But warmth was starting to creep into the space. In another hour it would be comfortable.

"I suppose Sam will be coming back from Florida soon," Charlene commented. She didn't appear anxious to get off the line and to be honest, I was relieved to chat with her while I waited for reinforcements to arrive.

"I suppose. Mary didn't say when he's coming." I sipped my coffee, wondering if I dared pump Charlene, She Who Knew All Town Gossip, about the owner. Oh, what the heck. Why not? "I've heard he's a tough boss. One of the kids said Sam was a bit intimidating."

I had yet to meet Sam Barlow, the co-owner of the business. His sister Mary, who lived year-round in Minnesota, hired me while Sam was doing his snowbird thing in Florida. Mary and her husband Joe Hannon were in charge of the landscape center while it ran on abbreviated hours between January and March. There was no need for full-time staff. Mary, Joe, me, and a couple of other students handled the greenhouses where we were growing Easter lilies and daffodils by the hundreds, along with the pansies and petunias we seeded a few weeks before. I loved going in there and seeing bench after bench full of tiny pots with miniscule green shoots just emerging.

"Sam? I suppose you could say he was intimidating, but I think he's what you could call focused." Charlene sounded doubtful.

"Really? In what way?"

"He's always been a serious person. I remember in high school, Sam never pulled any crazy stunts like the other boys. Of course, his father was a stickler for doing what's right. His father always cared about their standing in the community." Charlene sighed. "I suppose that's why Mary ran off to join the Peace Corps as soon as she graduated. I always thought it was unfair of her to have her adventures and leave Sam to take over the business. Hold on."

I heard the low murmur of voices then Charlene came back on the line. "Jake should be there right about now."

"I wonder if I should go out to the gate to meet him. I can turn on the exterior lights so he—" I paused, my coffee cup halfway to my lips. I heard the distinct sound of a door opening and closing. "Shit," I whispered. "Somebody just came in the back door." I set my coffee mug down carefully, barely breathing. Had I really heard a noise? It was so hard to tell over the noise from the ancient heaters overhead. I strained my ears, my loud heartbeat almost drowning out a faint scuffle sound. I looked around frantically. I was trapped in the small break room with no door in or out except the one in front of me.

No door, that is, except the door where I heard footsteps approaching.

Chapter 3

"Charlene, somebody's there." I went to the counter but the only weapon in sight was a plastic fork and the hot coffee. I hefted the pot, keeping the phone pressed to my ear. "Somebody's at the door."

"Hang on, Cassie, you just hang on." I heard Charlene talking excitedly to someone, presumably Jake at the other end of the police dispatch call unit.

Easy for her to say. Hang on to what? I backed up, the phone clutched in one hand and the coffee pot in the other. The door opened and a man looked into the room. My first thought was, 'This guy couldn't hurt a fly.' He had thick white and gray hair, cut short and sort of mussed around his square, tanned face. Pale gray-rimmed eyeglasses framed his dark eyes and his shoulders were hunched in a short waist-length leather jacket. He looked solidly built and not overly tall, maybe six-foot at the most.

His eyes widened when he saw me, coffeepot in hand as I glared at him. "Who are you?" he demanded, taking a step into the room.

"Who are you?" I raised the coffepot higher.

He stopped, correctly interpreting my threatening move. "The owner."

26

The answer was so unexpected it didn't register at first. "Say what?"

"The owner. Who are you?"

I lowered the coffeepot slightly. "Show me some I.D."

"I'm Sam Barlow," he said, sounding exasperated. "The owner."

"I heard you the first time. I'd like to see your I.D. How did you get in?"

Now he *looked* exasperated, too. "I own the place. I know how to get in and out."

I had one of those *well, duh* moments but I ignored it. "Why are you here so early in the morning?"

"I always come in and open."

"Yeah, well, Mary didn't tell me about it." I kept the coffeepot raised, but I was starting to believe him.

"Cassie?" A new voice echoed loudly in the main part of the shop.

"In here!" I set the coffeepot down, my hand trembling so bad I almost missed the burner. The pot clattered loudly as I got it settled in place.

The man looked over his shoulder. "Hey, Jake."

"Sam, I didn't know you were back in town."

I pulled out a folding chair and sat down, my knees rubbery and loose. "Was that you out on the street in the truck just now?"

The man—Sam—came into the room followed by Jake Caulfield, a short heavyset police officer whom I met at the Police Department Open House the year before, when the new station was completed.

"I just got back in town," Barlow said, going to the coffee counter and opening the cupboard above. He pulled out a chipped navy blue mug emblazoned with the Burpee Seed Company emblem.

"What truck?" Jake's cheeks were red with cold and he clanked when he walked, the police accoutrements dangling from his belt like charms from an oversized charm bracelet.

"There was a truck outside on the street, when I came in." I eyed Barlow as he filled his coffee mug. Something about him looked vaguely familiar but I was sure I had never met him. He had the craggy, weathered look of a man who worked outside and in the sun, not wrinkled so much as creased. He was probably about my age, maybe older, with a stocky, muscular build. "It was just sitting there, idling."

"Damn." Barlow's voice was low and husky, and it, too, seemed familiar. "I told Mary we should have a guy come in and open. It's not safe to have a woman here alone in the morning, especially with the trouble you've been having in town." He said this to Jake, like I wasn't sitting there, the object of his conversation. "I'll have to talk to her about it and—"

"Excuse me." I picked up my coffee mug, pleased my hand didn't shake. "As you can see, I'm fine. I told Mary I could open and I can. No problem."

Barlow's eyes narrowed as he stared at me over his own mug. "You're not fine if somebody is sitting out in a truck, watching you open."

"What are you doing here?" I demanded, more to change the subject than anything. "I thought you were in Florida."

"I got back on Tuesday night." He sipped his coffee, eyeing me curiously. "You look familiar. Have we met?"

"No. I started working here in February."

"I'll have a look around and make sure there's nobody outside," Jake said, pulling a black foot-long flashlight from his belt.

Barlow pushed away from the counter where he leaned. "I'll join you."

"And so will I," I said, getting up.

"You don't have to," Barlow said.

"It's my job to watch out for the place and I do

my job." I put my mug down and led the way out of the employee break room, not looking to see if the males were trailing behind me. This was going to put me behind in my chores for the morning. I had to get work wrapped up by nine then get across town to school for my first class at ten o'clock. The sooner we got started, the better.

Jake caught up to me as I reached the back door. "I'll go first," he said, brushing past me. I didn't argue. He was a cop, after all, and if there was a problem it was best he deal with it.

"Mary said she hired a student from Southern Minn Tech," Barlow said behind me.

I glanced back. He was closing the door to the main building, his shoulders hunched against the cold. "I am a student. I graduate in a few weeks."

"Change in careers?" He fell into step beside me as we followed Jake, walking between the potting greenhouse on our right and the bulb greenhouses on our left.

"You might say so. I was laid off a few years ago and decided to do something I enjoyed. You know what they say—the only way to make a dream come true is to wake up and live it."

"A dream come true? Working at a landscape company?" He dug his hands into his jacket pockets. I guessed he was cold, probably not acclimated yet from his cushy life in Florida during the winter.

I shrugged. "It beats sitting behind a desk or in meetings all day, the way I used to do." I paused as Jake jiggled the greenhouse doorknob. It didn't budge and he moved on, his flashlight beam adding to the illumination from the motion lights coming on as we walked.

"Is that what you did before? Sit in meetings?"

"Sometimes. I was a programmer and we always had design meetings or demos for customers. That reminds me. Mary said I should talk to you about something. I was thinking you should upgrade the computer system. There's new software out now that can tie into an inventory system and help with marketing." I paused again as Jake moved out of sight, walking behind the greenhouses and disappearing into the tree lot. "I got a demo copy and customized it. I think it might be useful."

Barlow stood next to me, his breath blowing white clouds into the air. "Is Ed Jenkins finally incorporating computers into his classes?" His voice sounded amused.

I glanced at him. "You know Ed?"

"Sure. I've been hiring kids out of his classes for years now. How's he doing?"

"Fine, although the excitement yesterday was—" That was when it hit me. I stared at Barlow, at the dark leather jacket, the hunched shoulders, the salt-and-pepper hair. "It was you," I said, taking a step back. "I saw you talking to Dr. Peavey in the greenhouse." I took another step away from him, prepared to run for Jake and safety if needed.

"You did?" Barlow looked curious, not worried, that I'd seen him. "I didn't see you there. Or wait...yeah, I think I did, didn't I? You were talking to Joe Swenson's kid in the hallway, right outside the potting room, right?"

"Who's Joe Swenson?" I looked past Barlow and saw Jake's flashlight bobbing back toward us from the end of the greenhouse. "Jake!" I hurried forward to meet him.

"Joe Swenson is Mike Peavey's business partner," Barlow said, his face puzzled as he followed after me. "We were all in college together."

I was almost running now, aiming straight for Jake. I barely heard Barlow's explanation as I focused on Jake and his flashlight.

"What's the big deal? What's the hurry?" Barlow called after me.

Damn. I had to tell the police my boss might be a potential murderer. What was the social etiquette for this situation? I decided to forget politeness and blurted, "Jake, the police are looking for him." I pointed a finger at Barlow, who stopped a few feet away and watched Jake and me, a bemused expression on his square face.

"Say what?" Jake shone his flashlight fully on Barlow, who turned his face away from the glare. The reflection on his eyeglasses gave him a momentary blind look, like Little Orphan Annie or Sandy, Annie's dog.

"The police, over in Roseville. They're looking for him. He was talking to Dr. Peavey right before he died." The words tumbled out and I was powerless to stop them. "I heard him threaten Dr. Peavey yesterday, in the greenhouse at the school."

"You were in the greenhouse?" Barlow asked, taking a step toward me.

I ducked behind Jake, who looked startled. I peered around him at Barlow. "I heard you two arguing. The police are looking for him." I looked up at Jake as I ducked back behind him.

Barlow took another step forward but Jake straightened and lifted the flashlight. "We heard about it down at the station. I knew they were looking for someone."

I peeked around his bulk. Barlow still didn't look worried or upset. He just looked puzzled. "Heard about what? Did something happen?"

"You know what happened," I said. "Dr. Peavey's dead."

Barlow's eyes widened. "What? Mike's dead? When?"

I stepped out from behind Jake, momentarily forgetting safety. "He was murdered yesterday, right when you saw him."

"That's impossible. He was fine when I left him."

"Well, he wasn't fine when I found him a few minutes later," I shot back. "He was lying on the floor and he was dead. He looked like he was poisoned."

"What?" Barlow looked shaken. Either he was a good actor or he really didn't know about Peavey.

His reaction wasn't my concern. I did my civic duty. I looked at Jake. "You have to arrest him or something."

"Arrest me for what? Arguing with someone? Hell, if I was arrested every time Mike Peavey and I argued, I'd have a criminal record as long as my arm."

"We need to get this cleared up, Sam," Jake said apologetically.

I glared at him, outraged. "Cleared up? What do you mean, 'cleared up'? The police want to talk to him because he was seen arguing with a man who was later found dead. That's a bit more than a clearing-up matter, if you ask me."

"Nobody asked you," Barlow snapped.

"Hey, don't get mad at me. I'm just doing my citizenly duty here."

Jake interposed himself between me and Barlow, who looked like he might take a swing at me. "I've known Sam most of his life, Cassie. I'm sure there's just a misunderstanding here. I'll contact the Roseville police and we'll get to the bottom of it." He gestured with his flashlight to the main building. "I didn't find anything out in the yard. Why don't you go inside? I'll call the station and have somebody come out and stay with you until the shop opens."

"I'm fine," I snapped. "I have to get to work." I glared at Barlow, who glared back at me, his hands jammed into his jacket. "I don't want my boss to think I'm derelict in my duties."

"I'm not your boss," he said. "Mary is."

I heard, implied in his voice, *For now, at least.*

****

"Cassie!"

I barely heard Mary Hannon over the sound of the water as I sprayed the daffodils. I shut off my sprinkler and approached her warily. Mary was a big-boned, husky woman, stocky like her brother with chin-length straight brown hair. Like the rest of us, she wore a Barlow's dark blue sweatshirt with the nursery logo on the front, faded blue jeans, and work boots. I liked Mary, but I barely knew her and wasn't sure what her reaction would be to my turning her brother in to the cops.

"I suppose you heard what happened," I said before Mary could speak. "I'm sorry, but I had to tell the police. They were looking for him."

Mary held up a hand. "I understand. Sam and Mike Peavey have argued for years, ever since their fuss with the patents and—" She broke off, looking embarrassment. "Well, there's some bad blood between them. The police would have contacted Sam even if you didn't see him."

"Really?" I figured I'd better look busy since she was paying my salary, meager though it was. I moved the water wand over the pots, drizzling the fertilizer-enriched water onto the dirt.

"Sure. There was that business about the plant research and Sheila."

"Sheila?" I dribbled some more water on the daffs, inching my way down the aisle.

"Sam's ex-wife, a bitch of the first degree, if you ask me." Mary pursed her lips as though deep in thought then she seemed to come to some decision. "It all has to do with Dad. Our father died about two months ago, down in Florida. Sam was there with him when he passed."

"I'm sorry," I said automatically, winding up the watering hose and tucking it back under the potting bench nearest the front door. "I didn't know. I just assumed Sam was a snowbird." I guiltily remembered my uncharitable thoughts earlier in the morning.

"Sam usually takes a month off after Christmas then goes to see Dad. He retired about ten years ago and moved south. The problem is that Dad didn't change his will. Or he thought he had, but I guess he didn't." Mary looked perplexed, her square, placid face taking on the look I occasionally saw on Houdini's face when a window appeared, separating him from the outside world. "It turns out when Dad sold the business to Sam and me he forgot to mention the land was still deeded to Sheila, Sam's ex-wife. Sheila's family owned this parcel of land years ago and I guess Dad just leased the property rights all this time."

"That's a problem," I agreed.

"So now we need to get it all straightened out." Mary fell into step with me as I slipped out the side door, closing it quickly behind me. The sun was up and in another hour it would be warm enough to work near the greenhouses without a jacket. But for now the late March temps made our breath fog the air as we went from the bulb greenhouse to the main building. I made a beeline for the employee area and my locker where I stowed my mini-bag containing my keys, wallet, phone, and other essentials.

"I was hoping you could help us," Mary said.

I paused inside the employee room door to look at her curiously. "Me? How?"

"You're related to C.R. Whittington."

It took a moment for me to parse what she said. "C.R...How did you know that?" I went to the lockers on the far side of the room.

"It was on your application for employment."

I forgot about that. I always used Charlie as a reference whenever I applied for anything because the Whittington family was so well known in the Twin Cities. I twirled the combination lock on my locker handle and jiggled it open. "I forgot I put him down on the form." I stuffed my work gloves into my work jacket pocket and hung it up, taking out my bag, good coat and good gloves from the locker.

"I was wondering if you could talk to him." When I started to speak, Mary hurried on, as though afraid of what I might say. "Sheila said we had to get a lawyer to talk to her lawyer. We were hoping if a lawyer like Whittington contacted her, she might be willing to at least sit down and discuss it."

Charlie's reputation as a high-powered contract lawyer stood me in good stead often in the past. It looked like it might help me again. "I'll talk to him and see what he says," I offered. "I can't make any promises, though." Mary looked so relieved I resolved to push Charlie about it and see if he would take their case. "Charlie and I are on good terms. I'll see what I can do." I jiggled the locker door again and as I did so, the bank of metal cabinets shifted. I jumped back as a tiny mouse body skittered from the dust under the lockers. "Ooh, icky."

Mary jumped, too. "Where did that come from?"

We both leaned over cautiously. "I don't know." I nudged the dusty gray body with my foot. It was stiff and unresponsive, looking almost mummified.

"Oh, damn." Mary hurried to the kitchen area and yanked open a cupboard door above the sink. "Damn."

I followed her, peering up at the cabinet. I could see the overturned metal containers and coffee filters in disarray. Mary pulled her garden gloves out of her back pocket and reached into the cupboard. "Those little vermin have been here," she said, her voice full of loathing. As she carefully pulled out the coffee filters, we could see the telltale droppings, little black rice shapes stark against the white filters. "We'll have to get exterminators in. We can't have mice in the cupboards here."

"I suppose it's inevitable," I said sympathetically. "We are out in the country and there's all the empty land around us."

"We've never had trouble before," she fumed, dumping the coffee filters into the wastebasket. "Sam is always careful to mouse-proof the doors and foundation before he leaves for the winter. Damn."

She looked so worried I touched her arm in commiseration. "What a drag."

"We'll have to get the health inspectors out here once we're done with it, too."

"Health inspectors? You don't serve food."

We both looked at the coffee pot. I wondered sickly if I had consumed mouse poop with my morning cup of joe, then quickly dismissed the thought. Carl would never have prepped the coffee with icky coffee filters.

Mary grimaced and grabbed the pot, dumping the coffee into the sink and setting the glass pot under the faucet. "Better I should call them than they get an anonymous tip again."

"Again?" I extracted my Jeep keys and started to move toward the door.

"Somebody called them a couple of weeks ago when you found those dead sparrows in the greenhouse. They inspected our pesticide and fungicide lockup but nothing was touched." Mary frowned. "I'd still like to know how those birds died."

The dozen birds I found under the potting benches in the central greenhouse remained a mystery. I shrugged. "No idea how it happened. Or how the water pipe froze or how the fans failed in the north greenhouse. I think we're having a run of bad luck." I went to the punch clock. "I'll give Charlie a call tonight."

"Are you two related?"

"Kind of. He's my ex-husband."

"And you're on good terms?" she asked incredulously.

I used my punching-out actions to hide the amusement I know I showed. "We grew up together. Charlie's one of my best friends." I caught her dumbfounded expression. "I know. It's hard to believe but it's true. I'll give him a call tonight and see what he says."

"I didn't think two people could get divorced and be on speaking terms."

"Charlie and I have been divorced for decades. Any animosity we felt has died down by now. Do you know the name of the lawyer Mrs. Barlow hired?"

"Mrs. Barlow?" Mary looked blankly at me then shook her head. "Oh, you mean Sheila. She's Mrs. Peavey now."

I dropped my timecard into its slot and turned to stare at her. "What?"

Mary nodded, her bobbed hair moving forward to hide her face briefly. "I'm afraid so. Sheila was married to Sam but she left him for Mike about ten years ago." She sighed. "So you see, the police would talk to Sam no matter what you said. If anybody had a reason to kill Mike Peavey, Sam surely did."

Chapter 4

The fact that Sam Barlow's ex-wife was married to the victim added a layer of complexity to an already messy situation. I thought it over as I drove to school but in a matter of minutes my thoughts drifted ahead to my upcoming exams and to Grandy Theo's funeral on Saturday. The Barlow family troubles receded into the back of my brain as I drank deeply of chilly spring air and considered my short-term future.

April was almost on us and like the seasons turning, I was launching into a new phase of my life. I popped Judy Collins into the CD player and practiced my song for Saturday's funeral. I'd been called on to sing at Whittington family events for decades but I never performed this song in front of an audience, so I wanted to be spot-on for Grandy, who was—had been—one of my dearest friends. She was ninety-two when she died and sharp as a tack until the end, succumbing finally to a heart attack in the night. I would miss her trenchant humor and biting wit but I was happy for her that she went quickly and with dignity. My first Saturday afternoon of the month, which I tried to spend at least partly with her at our 'tea party,' would never be the same.

I allowed myself a few minutes of sniffling then banished my gloomy thoughts. Grandy would never forgive me for giving in to the blues. Her philosophy was 'living well really is the best revenge.' Being sad just wasn't part of her outlook on life, so I swiped away my tears.

I found a parking spot close to the school building and raced into the side entrance. I tossed my gear into my locker and slid into my seat just as Ed Jenkins walked into the Plant Propagation class, mug of coffee in hand and papers hanging out of the folder tucked under his arm. As usual, I sat with a couple of members of the Elder Ladies League near the front of the room.

"You found a body yesterday?" Barb Torvald hissed at me as I pulled out my notebook, pen, and textbook from my book bag.

"In the greenhouse," I whispered.

"Wow. I want the details at lunch. I can't believe I missed it."

I nodded as Ed launched into his lecture on grafting techniques for fruit trees. As soon as class was over, Barb and I headed for our lockers where we stowed our books and grabbed lunch bags. "Was he dead when you found him?" She stared at the greenhouse door now decorated with yellow Crime Scene tape. Her wide eyes and bug-eyed gaze told me she was worried something might jump out at us. Barb was a nervous person who claimed delicate health, but I've seen her wrestle a one hundred pound tree into place without breaking a sweat. I guess there are all kinds of delicate.

"I heard he was a bigwig or something," Mary Ellen Samuels said as she joined us. She was a tall, lanky woman who used to be an accountant.

"He was the speaker at the greenhouse

dedication," I said. "Apparently he and my boss knew each other."

"Your boss? Sam Barlow?" Barb led the way out of the Horticulture wing and into the main commons area of the school. "I've heard he's good looking."

I thought about Barlow and shrugged. "I guess so, in an older guy kind of way."

Mary Ellen laughed. "That's the best kind, isn't it?"

"Oh, I don't know, a young guy might be fun," Barb said as we wended our way through the crowded tables outside the cafeteria. She waved to the other ELLs sitting near the entrance. "I didn't bring lunch so I'm going to get a salad. Don't give any details until I get back."

I pulled out a chair and sat down, setting my thermos and lunch bag on the table. Then I remembered the mouse droppings back at the store and decided to forgo the coffee, just in case. As we ate our lunches I told the ELLs about the argument I heard and the surprising revelation that the arguing party who left the greenhouse alive was my boss, Sam Barlow.

"Holy shit," Donna said. "You might be working for a murderer."

I pulled out my three Oreo cookies and lined them up next to coffee I bought in the cafeteria. I allowed myself these three indulgences for lunch every day and I enjoyed every morsel. "He didn't strike me as a murderer." I separated the first cookie and licked off the frosting before nibbling the crunchy wafers. I sighed with pleasure then followed up with a sip of java.

"How many murderers do you know?" Barb asked.

"Good point," I admitted.

"Hey, Gidget."

I looked up at Aaron Swenson as he paused near

our table. "Hey, Aaron." Then I remembered my conversation earlier with Sam Barlow. "I didn't know you knew Dr. Peavey. He works with your dad, right?"

Aaron's eyes widened and for a minute he looked comically startled. Then he smiled but it didn't reach his blue eyes, which were red-rimmed and troubled. "They used to work together. My dad doesn't work at Min-Gen anymore." He eyed the other women at the table then leaned closer to me. "I heard they arrested Sam Barlow today." He had an odd way of talking, his voice very soft with pauses every three or four words. It had the effect of making me try to anticipate his next phrase.

"I don't think so." I pulled apart my second cookie then started licking the sweet white center. "The last I heard, they were just going to talk to him."

"Speaking of which..." He leaned even closer. "Can we talk?"

"Sure." I finished the second cookie and reached for the third.

"In private?"

I paused in mid-sip of coffee. "Uh, sure." I stood up. "We can go over there." I nodded toward a group of tables a few feet away and he moved off.

"What's up?" Susan asked.

I shrugged. "Private consultation." I trailed after Aaron, cookie in hand. "What's up?" I dropped into the nearby chair and started on my final Oreo.

"I've got a problem and I was hoping you could help." He stared down at the tabletop, his handsome face troubled. Now that we were closer, I saw that he looked exhausted, his eyes sunken, as though he hadn't slept much lately. He tapped on the table, an anxious staccato rhythm keeping time with his bobbing leg.

"What's wrong, Aaron?" I put a hand on his arm

to stop him. He stopped, but I felt tenseness under his denim shirt. "What's happened?"

"It's my...girlfriend," he said in a rush. "We have a problem."

Girlfriend? I released him and leaned back, chewing my cookie slowly. I didn't remember seeing Aaron with a girl before or after any classes. "Do I know her?" I asked cautiously. "Is she in school with us?"

"No, she's older. She's not in school."

"How much older?"

"That's not the problem." He resumed tapping the table. I felt the vibration through the floor as his foot bounced up and down. It exhausted me just to hear it. "I'm not sure how to explain it. I think I've got a big problem."

"What kind of problem?" Then I had a terrible thought. "She's not pregnant, is she? I can't advise you on something like that, Aaron. That's a personal choice a person has to make."

He smiled shakily. "No, I'm pretty sure she's not pregnant."

"You used something, didn't you?" I blushed, suddenly realizing what we were talking about, but I forged ahead anyway. "I mean, you used a condom or something, didn't you?"

"No." His nervous worry was replaced by surprise. "No, I didn't. I just assumed she would use something. You know, that she was on the pill or..."

"Oh, for cryin' out loud. You've got to use condoms in today's world. They aren't just for birth control, you know."

He looked embarrassed. "I can't go in and buy them. I mean, you have to show an I.D. and everything."

I blew out an exasperated breath. "Embarrassment is the least of your worries, Aaron."

He shook his head. "It's not that."

"Then what is it?" I moderated my tone. His potential run-in with a sexually transmitted disease really wasn't my business. "What's the problem?"

"I think she may have done something illegal."

I sat back and blinked widely. "Say what?"

Aaron stood up abruptly. "I shouldn't have said anything. I'm sorry. Forget I mentioned it. I shouldn't have told you—"

I sprang to my feet, too. "Aaron, if you're in trouble, you need to talk to the police or..." I thought frantically. "I don't know. There must be somebody you can talk to. What about your father?"

He laughed bitterly. "My father hates—" He *almost* said her name. I could see it as he started to form the word then he bit back whatever he was going to say. "He hates her. He blames her for everything that happened."

"What happened?"

"I shouldn't have said anything. I can't talk about it." He walked away, shoulders hunched as he scowled at the floor.

I stared after him. I'd only known Aaron for a few brief months, but he was always a sunny kid, cheerful and upbeat. This gloomy, morose stranger was odd and worrying.

"What was that all about?" Susan asked when I rejoined them.

I tidied up my lunch things, jamming my wax paper into my paper bag. "I don't know. He's worried about something but I couldn't get any details."

"Teenagers," Donna said with the voice of maternal experience. "It's probably about a girl. He's probably not sure if she really loves him or he's worried she's interested in some other guy or..." She shrugged. "You name it. His hormones have him all in an uproar."

"Maybe." I looked across the open space where Aaron was striding toward the hallway leading to the Horticulture wing and the classrooms there.

"I'm surprised he's working at Barlow's," Laurie said as she tucked her thermos into her pink thermal lunch bag. "I heard Sam Barlow doesn't like teenagers working there."

"Really?" I jerked my attention back to the resident queen of the ELL. Laurie had a lot of contacts in the gardening and landscaping community and was often an invaluable font of gossip. "Why does he feel that way, do you know?"

"He said they're too undependable." Laurie smiled thoughtfully. "It'll be awkward, I guess, working with somebody you turned in to the police."

I had a brief qualm at the thought. That would be awkward. "Oh, I probably won't see much of him. He's usually in the Roseville store."

"He and Mary Hannon take turns running the different stores. I heard they think it gives them a fresh approach to the two locations. I thought this year was his year to run the Pickaway store." Laurie picked up her Claiborne book bag and slung it over one shoulder.

"Well, you'd better hope he's not running the store where you're working," Susan said as she tidied up her lunch papers. "Joan said he has a hell of a temper."

I smiled weakly. "Good thing for me I probably won't ever see him again."

Those words came back to haunt me three hours later when Sam Barlow showed up at my townhouse door.

****

"Can you tell me why you told the police I threatened Mike Peavey?"

I had just stepped out of my Jeep with my arms full of bags: school bag, lunch bag, hand bag, and grocery bag. I didn't notice the man sitting in the SUV at the curb among the other cars parked on the street. I was too busy cursing the fact I misplaced my garage door opener and was now fumbling for my front door keys. I was tired, hungry and in no mood for an angry Sam Barlow who appeared at my side just as the motion light came on over the door. The groceries began a precarious slide and he caught them just in time.

"What are you doing?" I demanded, jamming my key in the lock and trying to wedge everything else I was carrying under one arm. "Give me that." I waggled my hand in the general direction of the grocery sack.

"Just get the door open," he snapped. "I'm not trying to steal your cat food."

"How did you know I lived here?" I made a futile grab for the groceries as I pushed open the door with my hip.

"You work for me, remember? I know your address. Get the door open and—whoa, do you want your cat out here?"

I dropped my lunch bag as Houdini lunged for the open door. "Shit, he's not supposed to go out. I just moved here and he'll get lost."

Barlow thrust my groceries at me, scooped up fourteen pounds of wriggling cat and grabbed the groceries back from me before I knew what happened. He pushed past me into the foyer and kept going, heading for the kitchen to the left of the entryway. "You want the groceries here?"

I nudged my lunch bag into the foyer and slammed the door behind me. "I didn't invite you in," I pointed out as I readjusted the remaining bags in my arms. I kicked off my shoes and followed him into the kitchen.

He put the groceries on the counter and set Houdini on the floor. "No, but he did." Barlow straightened up, looking around. "Nice place. You get a lot of good light here."

Trust a man who ran a nursery to notice the southern exposure even when it was seven at night and the sun was setting. I dropped my book bag on the tiny dining room table. "Mr. Barlow, I don't feel comfortable having you here. I think you should leave."

"*You* don't feel comfortable?" He turned from his inspection of my window and leaned against the kitchen island separating the cooking area from the eating area, his arms crossed on his chest. "How comfortable do you think I felt when the police questioned me?"

I straightened indignantly. "That's unfair. I was asked some questions and I answered them." I turned to the grocery sack and began pulling items out. "Now I think you should leave. I don't think it's right a witness is talking to..." *a suspect*, I thought but didn't say.

"You weren't a witness to anything. All you heard was me and Mike Peavey arguing. We argued all the time." He watched as I unloaded the sack, his craggy face impassive.

"About your wife?" The words slipped out before I could stop them. I jammed the box of cat food into the cupboard to hide my embarrassment.

He narrowed his eyes and glared at me. They were a dark brown color, almost black, and contrasted sharply with his white and gray hair. "What about Sheila?"

I shrugged and used grocery-putting-away as an excuse to avoid his gaze. "Everyone knows she left you for Dr. Peavey."

"Everyone knows?"

I looked at him over my shoulder as I slid a plastic bottle of tomato juice into the cupboard. "Or so I've heard."

"Don't believe everything you heard." He looked at Houdini, who wended his way around my feet in an intricate feline dance. "Big cat."

"Mr. Barlow, I don't think you should be here. I doubt if the police—"

"Sam."

I toed Houdi out of the way and pulled the bags of cheese and a box of frozen spinach out of the bottom of the grocery sack. "I don't think it would be appropriate for me to call you by your first name."

"All my employees do."

He watched me with an unwavering stare as I arranged the items on the counter. "I still don't think it's right that you're here talking to me. The police might think—"

"I've been cleared. What are you doing?"

I pulled mushrooms out of the sack. "I'm getting ready to cook." I looked at the clock. The meager lunch I ate seven hours earlier was a distant memory. I had supper to make and my breakfast quiches to get done. Then his words soaked in. "What do you mean, you've been cleared?"

"Mike ingested whatever killed him hours before he died. He told several people he didn't feel well and apparently the police tested his blood and found...whatever in it. I couldn't have killed him."

"So? Why does it mean you're cleared? Perhaps you..." Barlow was shaking his head. "What?" I set the box of frozen spinach in the sink to thaw.

"I got into town late Tuesday night and spent most of Wednesday morning at the Barlow's store in Roseville." When I started to speak he overrode me. "I have witnesses. It wasn't me who killed Mike Peavey."

"What did kill him? I saw blood."

"Blood?" He straightened and regarded me with those alert dark eyes. "Where?"

Oops. Maybe I shouldn't have mentioned that little detail. Damn. The police didn't specifically say what I should and shouldn't discuss, but I think it

47

was implied. "On the floor," I said vaguely. "Perhaps he keeled over and hit his head on the bench or something."

"What did he look like?"

"I beg your pardon?"

"What were his symptoms? If he had dilated pupils and a rigid face, it might be jasmine or narcissus. It's the right time of year. Well, it's too early for the poison part of jasmine. That's the berries. It'll be a while before it's poisonous, all we've got is the plant right now. We've got pots of narcissus everywhere. The bulb there is deadly. The poison can act almost instantaneously depending on the amount ingested or it might take a few hours, depending on if it was ground up...Or it might be bloodroot. It can take hours to kill. Symptoms of bloodroot poisoning are vomiting and...No, wait. You didn't say he vomited." Sam frowned. "You'd notice if it was bloodroot. It's pretty violent. How about—?" He shook his head. "Most plant poisons cause vomiting or diarrhea. It must have been a chemical."

I swallowed hard. His knowledge was impressive. "How do you know so much about it?" I managed to ask.

"Work with me here. What were his symptoms? Cyanosis? Dermatitis? Were his limbs fixed and rigid? Was he curled in a fetal ball? What about—" He must have noticed the shocked look on my face. "What?"

"How do you know so much about it?"

He looked at my book bag, the contents spilled onto my faux oak kitchen table. The *Guide to Pesticide and Herbicide Applications* was on top of the stack, its bright orange cover visible from several feet away. "I took the state certification test, too. In fact, I've taken it every year for the last three decades. I'm licensed to dispense poisonous chemicals. I get re-certified every year." He raised his eyes and looked directly into mine. "I know all about poison."

Damn.

Had Donna been right?

Was I working for a murderer?

Chapter 5

I cleared my throat and considered the knife block. I could grab one if needed and use it to defend myself. Or I could—

Oh, who was I kidding? I couldn't stab him unless he was coming after me with a Norman Bates look on his face and muttering *Mother,* with his hands curled into rigid claws, ready to grab me. The man standing in front of me was watching me with polite curiosity, like I was a moron he was humoring. He may have been a consummate actor, but I'd bet he wasn't a murderer.

"I didn't stay to examine him closely," I admitted. "He had a bluish tint to his face and his hands were..." I looked away. "He looked sick," I finished. I nudged the spinach box with one finger but of course, it hadn't thawed yet. So much for using that as a diversion.

There was a long silence. When I looked at him again, Sam Barlow was regarding me with a sympathetic expression. He cleared his throat and continued. "The police didn't tell me but whatever it was, it was probably given to him earlier in the day or maybe the night before." He glanced down at

Houdini, who sat in the middle of the floor, staring implacably at me. "Is it his dinnertime, too?"

"It's always food time for a cat." I went into the laundry room/pass-through that separated the kitchen from the garage and busied myself with Houdi's food dishes, returning to find Sam Barlow, who hadn't budged an inch. "Is there something else you wanted to talk to me about besides my desire to do my civic duty?"

His stern, unyielding features wavered slightly and he almost smiled. "Mary wanted me to look over the prototype computer program you were customizing for us. She said you had it running on your home computer?"

"Yes, I do, but..." I glanced at the clock.

He ignored my subtle hint and continued watching me, his gaze unwavering. "I'd like to look it over so we can implement it as soon as possible. Will it take long to show me how it's set up? Maybe you can give me an idea of what it looks like. It sounds like an interesting program."

"I have some documentation I put together. I can print it out and you can take it with you." I started toward the living room then looked down at his shoes. "Do you mind?"

"Sorry. I was more worried about grabbing the runaway than I was about the linoleum." He went back to the foyer and kicked off his boots. Houdi immediately abandoned his food to examine Barlow's footwear, his face almost disappearing into the large opening of the shoe. Barlow regarded him with a bemused expression on his craggy face. "What's his name?"

"Houdini." I brushed past Barlow and went into the miniscule den situated off the front entry of my townhouse.

"Apt name for him." Barlow padded after me, his socked feet making no sound on the hard wood floors. "Am I interrupting your supper?"

"I haven't started it yet so you aren't interrupting." I sat down at my door-on-crates desk and clicked the mouse to deactivate the screen saver, a slow-motion depiction of a rose in bloom. "I set it up according to your sister's specifications," I said as I clicked the icon with the large dollar sign.

Barlow pulled over a chair and sat, peering past me at the screen. "You've got mail."

I ignored the little flashing mailbox icon. "I always have mail. I set up the program to—"

"Aren't you going to check it?"

I looked to my left. His face was about a foot from mine and he was staring intently at the computer screen. I could see the little spikes of whisker on his cheeks and how his eyes wrinkled as he smiled. Oh. He was smiling. At me. I jerked my eyes away from his and looked at the screen, my ears hot with embarrassment at being caught staring. "It's probably nothing important," I muttered, clicking the mailbox icon.

Surprise her with your new enlarged Man Stick.

"Oh, for cryin' out loud," I muttered. "I need to refine my SPAM filter."

Barlow looked at the message on the screen and grinned. "Man stick. That's a good one."

I rolled my eyes. "Good Lord, why does penis length get such air time? Men and their penises. I don't understand it."

"We're sort of attached, if you know what I mean."

"I'm attached to my boobs but it doesn't mean I have to spam the world with ads to have them enhanced."

Barlow's eyes flickered to my bosom. I wasn't as petite on my top half as I wanted to be since being 38-29-36 and only five-foot-three makes me a bit conspicuous. "Well, it's a bit more important for a man, I guess," he drawled. "After all, we provide the equipment."

"Aren't you egocentric?" I muttered. I deleted the email then saw the subject on the next one in the queue. I clicked it open, scanning the contents. *Charlie left me because of you. I don't know what you told him, but I'll never forgive you for ruining our relationship.* "Damn. I need to tell Charlie about this."

"Charlie? He's the lawyer my sister talked about?" Barlow glanced at me then back at the screen.

I tore my eyes away from the screen and nodded distractedly. "Yes." I opened the folder containing the test programs I set up for Barlow Nurseries. "As you can see, Mr. Barlow, I set this up so you can use point of sales to—"

"Sam."

I considered several replies and finally settled for, "Okay. Sam. I set these up so we can use point of sales to track inventory. It's all tied in to the bar code system used when plants are potted at the nursery." I pointed to the screen, which I customized to match the way items were grouped at Barlow's Landscape Center. "We'll need to refine the bar coding slightly. Right now we lump all the annuals together into one category, but I think we'll want to sort them by type, don't you?"

"So what did you hear yesterday in the greenhouse that made you think I was threatening Mike Peavey?"

I leaned back in my chair and swiveled to regard Barlow. The movement almost dumped me onto his lap since he was relaxed back in his chair, his denim-clad legs stretched out near mine, our feet sharing the crowded space under my desk. "Did you come over here to look at the inventory program or to talk about the greenhouse incident?"

"The greenhouse incident? You make it sound like an international thriller or something." He looked at the white bookshelves lining the walls above the desk in the small room. "You must read a lot." He stretched and snagged a book from the shelf.

I almost groaned aloud when I saw the title. What perverse little twist of fate had put *Love's Savage Passion* into Sam Barlow's hot big hands? The heroine on the cover had hair as long as the hero's, whose muscles rippled just as the wind rippled his hair. I kept the book for its amusement value and for the hot sex scenes, which fueled my imagination on a few sleepless nights.

"As a matter of fact I do read a lot." I grabbed for the book but he casually turned aside, putting the book out of my reach.

"This looks like an old favorite." He opened it and skimmed the page as I watched, fuming. "My, my. Who knew they wrote such things?"

"I haven't had time to sort my books properly yet." I gave up on grabbing the book, turning back to the computer screen. I clicked open the documentation I had assembled which described the original software program, the minor changes I made, and the operating instructions. "I'll print this for you and you can take it with you." I leaned past him to check the printer, making sure it was stocked with paper.

"Hmm?" He looked up from the book, his dark eyes innocently curious. "Sorry. This book really caught my attention. Can I borrow it?"

I snatched it from his grasp. "No." I clicked the *print* icon and the printer whirred into life, paper sliding smoothly out of its maw.

"So what did you hear that had you so convinced I was a killer?"

The bantering, easy-going tone was gone from his voice. A cold-eyed businessman stared at me now. "Why do you want to know?" I asked slowly.

"Because you may have overheard confidential information."

"Then you shouldn't talk in a public place." He put a hand on my wrist and I stared down at it then at him. "Let go of me."

He immediately released me. "I'm sorry. It's just...Mike and I talked about some things that I don't want to be public knowledge."

I shot to my feet. "I'm not in the habit of gossiping about what I overhear."

"Really? What about that crack you made about 'everybody knows about Sheila and Mike?' That sounds like gossip to me."

I glared down at him, hands on my hips. "Your sister told me that."

"My sis—" He frowned. "I should have known."

"Hey, she was defending you. Don't complain." I leaned over him and pulled the paper off the printer tray. "Here's the spec sheet I wrote. I'm also printing the rest of the documentation I put together. You can review it and if you have questions, we can—"

"I'm sorry. It's just..." He rubbed tiredly at the bridge of his nose, his glasses riding up and settling back down in the little groove they made. "Mike and I were talking about some confidential stuff that might cost me a lot of money. I'm worried, that's all."

I straightened slowly, conscious I was only a few inches away from him. I tried to sit back down, almost tipping over as the chair skittered away underneath me. "Damn," I muttered.

He steadied me with a hand on my waist. "Careful."

I flopped into my chair, surprised by the rush of heat I experienced at his touch. It was a long time since a man had been this close to me. I was obviously out of practice with the experience. "I heard the entire conversation. I was in the back, cleaning up the potting benches. I couldn't hear every word because the ventilation fans kept kicking on, but when you moved into the center of the greenhouse, I could hear clearly."

His forehead wrinkled in thought. "So you heard about the patent lawsuit and the stock options and all?"

I nodded. "Were you really going to sue the University of Minnesota for patent infringement?" I'd been thinking about this for the past day and was curious about his reply.

He leaned forward and rested his elbows on his knees, his hands clasped between his legs. Houdi took this as an invitation to schmooze and promptly rubbed against the hands, his back arching and tail flicking to indicate This Was A Good Thing. Sam absently dug his fingers into the thick yellow fur, scratching my portly cat behind his ears and eliciting a paroxysm of purring that nearly drowned out the printer. "Yeah, I was looking into it. Mary said your hotshot lawyer might be able to help."

"I don't know if Charlie knows about patent law. He's a contract lawyer." I glanced at the photograph on my desk of me and Charlie, arms around each other as we sat on his sailboat one autumn day out on Lake Minnetonka.

Sam's gaze followed mine and he frowned. "Mary said you were divorced."

"I am." I started to reach toward the printer but he beat me to it, pulling pages off and handing them to me. "Charlie and I are good friends," I said as I shuffled the paper. "Do you want me to check with him tomorrow and see if he knows any patent attorneys?" I sorted the pages in my hand and held them out, surprising a look of assessment on Sam's face that was a bit disconcerting. "Is something wrong?"

"You're not what I expected." He took the pages,

staring down at them as he still leaned over. Houdi, of course, viewed this as an excellent game and poked at the paper with his nose, play peek-a-boo and generally being a nuisance.

"What were you expecting?" I leaned back and nudged my yellow feline with one toe. Delighted with the attention, he promptly lay down and stretched, displaying a plump belly that demanded a rub.

"I'm not sure. So you heard me and Mike arguing and you figured I killed him?"

I blew out an exasperated sigh. "No, I didn't figure you killed him. I just told the police that as far as I knew, you were the last person to see him alive. What kind of patent lawsuit are you talking about?"

Sam stared down at the pages in his hand, his eyelashes dark and long on his face. A woman would kill for lashes like that. Then he raised his head and looked at me. His dark eyes were hard but softened when he saw my sympathetic look. Maybe that's what made him decide to confide in me.

"I went to college late in life, after I got out of the service. When I was there Mike and I worked on a couple of botany projects together. Even though he was younger than me, we were good friends." His eyes took on the vacant look of memory. "He and Sheila were the same age and in the same classes. She was in botany then, too. That's how we met." His expression hardened. "Mike was into the chemistry and I was into the plant sciences. We developed some promising hybrid azaleas."

I nodded in understanding. Developing cold-hardy plants for Minnesota and other northern climates was a lucrative pastime but it took a lot of time, money, talent, and effort. Developing the plants was only part of the equation. Marketing, research, and testing occupied a large percentage of any budget. "So what happened?"

"To make a long story short, Mike lied to me. He said the hybrid we developed didn't have potential." Sam's eyes once again got that hard, distant look. "Imagine my surprise when I saw 'Sheila's Sunrise' discussed in last February's issue of *The Northern Gardener.*"

"Wow." I blinked in surprise. "That azalea got quite a write-up. It was yours?" *The Northern Gardener* was a magazine that went to all members of the Minnesota Horticultural Society. Because of that, any plants discussed in it were instantly in the marketing spotlight.

He nodded, finally straightening up and leaning back, still holding the documentation I printed for him. "I'm going to get a sample and test it, but yeah, I'm sure it's based on the stock we developed in college."

I nodded slowly. It took years to develop a new plant, especially if one did it the old-fashioned way by grafting and pollination as opposed to the scientific way of gene manipulation. Most growers couldn't afford the lab facilities genetic modification required and relied on the tried and true, albeit slower, methods. "It could be worth some money."

"It's not just the money." Sam stared down at Houdi, draped on my foot, and the angry look on his face softened. "It's the..."

Understanding rushed through me. He created that plant for his wife then both she and the plant were taken from him. The poor man. I never loved anyone enough to create a plant for them. True, I loved Charlie and still did, but I had never been *in love* with him. Poor Sam Barlow loved and lost the woman he held most dear.

Add to the insult the fact that the item he'd created for her was stolen as well and was now being sold by his biggest enemy. It was no wonder he was so angry. "I can see why you were shouting at him."

He glanced at me. "Most women would say it's just a plant."

I snorted. "And a rose is just a rose. We know better." Our eyes met and for an instant I felt as though we were in perfect harmony with each other, looking deeply into our individual souls. Then Houdi tapped the pages in Sam's hands and the moment vanished. "I really didn't hear much more. I did hear something about stock options. You were demanding to be given options in his company, right?"

Sam nodded. "It seems only fair. After all, it was my work that helped create some of the products his company is producing." He frowned down at the inventory information he held. "We can use the money. I'd like to invest it back in the business." Then he looked up at me guiltily, as though suddenly aware he shared personal information with a total stranger.

"That makes sense to me," I agreed, standing up carefully so I didn't tread on Houdi or Sam, both watching me with similar alert, hopeful looks. "I can stop by the office tomorrow and talk about it if you like," I volunteered, gesturing to the papers he held.

Sam stared at me for a second or two longer then stood. "I'd appreciate it if you could. I think this will be useful and if we can implement it as soon as possible, I want to do it."

My mail icon pinged and I leaned over, clicking open the mailbox. *You deserve not to be ignored by women.* "It sounds like a fortune cookie," I said with a laugh.

He grinned, the little fans around his eyes deepening. "Well, as long as the right woman pays attention, I guess it doesn't matter." He stared down at me, his eyes suddenly dark and mysterious. "Right?"

I may have been out of practice with men, but even I could see the invitation in his dark eyes.

Chapter 6

I was so flustered I almost toppled over backward. "Indeed. Of course." I was babbling but I couldn't control the words slipping out. "Now if you'll excuse me, I have to—I have some food and—I'm going to—"

"Sure. Sorry I interrupted your evening." Sam sidled past me, stepping over Houdi and brushing by me where I was rooted to the spot. "Can you meet me tomorrow in the afternoon? Are you working after class?"

I struggled to remember what I was doing on the morrow. "Yes, I am. So any time after two o'clock would be fine."

He pulled out a Blackberry. "That'll work. I might be a few minutes late."

I watched in fascination as he thumbed in a notation. He looked up and saw my impressed look. "I've always wanted one of those," I confessed. "I'm a gadget junkie."

Sam grinned. "So am I. I keep upgrading. Someday I'll say 'enough', but..." He slipped the shiny little phone into his pocket. "Not yet." He went to the foyer and put on his boots. I realized to my chagrin he still wore his leather jacket. I hadn't even asked if he wanted to take it off. Then I remembered he practically forced his way into my house and my guilty feeling evaporated.

He straightened up and opened the door. I grabbed Houdi, whose fascination with this strange new world hadn't abated. "Thanks for catching him the first time."

Sam rubbed Houdi's head and I was rewarded by claws in my arms. "It was probably my fault he got out in the first place." Sam's eyes met mine. "Sorry I burst in like that."

"It's okay. I'm just settling in for a night of studying anyway."

He tilted his head to one side in thought. "Finals?"

I nodded.

"Don't worry about the pesticide licensing exam," he said in a low, confiding voice. "It's a piece of cake."

"Maybe for you. You've got years in the business."

"A little common sense goes a long way, in pesticide application and in life." He held up the papers in his right hand. "Thanks for this. I'll look it over tonight."

I nodded and started to close the door behind him. He paused and looked back at me then continued walking down my sidewalk that was edged with daffodils just starting to emerge.

I closed the door and let Houdi slip from my arms. He immediately went to the den window to peer out at his disappearing buddy. After a moment's debate I joined him, peeking out to see Sam Barlow getting into a dark maroon SUV. "What'ja think, Houdi?"

He hopped to the floor and went to the kitchen, obviously done with socializing and ready to move on to more important things, such as eating. I joined him, soon busy with making my breakfast quiches and finally sitting on the couch with a ham sandwich at eight o'clock.

Of course, as soon as I sat down I realized I was still missing my garage door opener. I considered postponing a search for it, but I remembered Sam Barlow's words about common sense. If I had a disappeared garage door opener, I needed to find it. I went back out to my car and drove it into the garage then searched under the seats, pulling up the mats to check.

No opener. I also checked the glove compartment and the trash bag. No opener. I closed and locked the garage door then went back into the house, closing and locking the access door behind me. Sandwich in hand, I went to all the logical spots inside the house, checking my book bag, lunch bag, purse, and finally turning to the remaining boxes stored in the back bedroom.

No opener. "Damn," I said to Houdi who followed me into the room to continue his endless exploration of the Land of the Boxes. I had changed the opener frequency when I moved into the townhouse weeks before, so the process was still fresh in my mind. I trudged back to the garage, grabbing the spare opener from the Everything Totally Confused drawer where I tossed it upon moving in. A few minutes later I reprogrammed it and once again had a garage door opener. I put the spare into my Jeep and went back inside.

As I passed the front window I saw a car driving by slowly on the cul-de-sac's road in front of the house. I turned off the kitchen light and went into the den. I started to shut down my computer for the night but my open mailbox icon reminded me. I picked up the phone and called Charlie, who answered on the third ring.

"What's up, Cassie? Have you recovered from finding the dead body in the greenhouse?"

"I think so, although I did have some nightmares about it. I'm glad the cops decided the school wasn't at fault. They can't afford the bad publicity."

"No kidding. Not to mention the lawsuits. I did some checking. Peavey had a three-million dollar grant in the works for the University of Minnesota, doing research into some kind of new plant or something. And he also had a grant pending at your school. That one was only for a million bucks. Yeah, he'll be missed."

"Really? You talked to people who knew him?"

"No. But anybody who brings in millions to an institution will be missed." Charlie's voice was wry. "Trust me. I know these things."

"That's one of the reasons I'm calling, Charlie." I told him about my conversation with Sam Barlow and my earlier conversation with Mary Hannon. "Can you help them?" I asked hopefully.

"You mean with the contract stuff? Probably. I'm not sure about the patent infringement, though. You'll want a specialist for patent law. Let me check around my law firm. I might know somebody who can help."

"Thanks, Charlie. Maybe I can get Sam Barlow off my back if I can find him some legal help." I looked at my computer screen. "There's something else. I got an email tonight." I clicked open my SPAM folder but the earlier email was gone. "Damn. It was in my SPAM bucket and it must have been deleted. My mail program cleans out the folder on a regular basis."

"What kind of email?"

"I'm pretty sure it was from Kathleen. Your Kathleen," I added in case he wasn't sure who I meant. "Sam Barlow was here and I just glanced at it." I checked the Trash folder on my email system but as I suspected the letter wasn't there. The SPAM junk was automatically deleted, not routed to the Trash folder like my other email. "She said something about how she blamed me for your relationship ending." I wracked my brain, trying to remember the exact wording.

"Oh, for Pete's sake," Charlie snapped. "How did she get your email address? No, wait. I know. When we had that party last year she asked for everybody's email address so she could send out the pictures afterward. Damn it."

"I think you're going to need to talk to her. I don't think she understands."

He laughed ruefully. "Nobody does. We have a unique relationship."

I thought of Mary Hannon and Sam Barlow's disbelief that I could be friends with my ex-husband. "We had a unique childhood." There was a long pause and I know Charlie's memories were coinciding with mine. "You saved my life," I said softly.

"And you saved mine," he replied, equally softly. "I tried to explain to Kathleen but..."

I knew what he meant. Whenever I described my connection to the Whittingtons, I was usually met with disbelief. I gave up trying and now just resorted to facile clichés. "You need to talk to her, Charlie."

He sighed. "I'll try. She was upset, though. Maybe I'll try in a day or two." I started to protest but he didn't let me speak. "I have to go out to the south metro tomorrow afternoon on business. Why don't I stop at Barlow's and talk to your boss about the contract thing. Will she be around?"

"I'll check in the morning and call you if she won't be there. What time?

"Hold on...I should be able to wrap up my

meeting by three o'clock. Three-thirty?"

I made a note on a scrap of paper on the desk. "Sounds good. I'll see you then."

"Cassie?"

"Hmm?"

He paused. "Nothing. I'll see you tomorrow."

I hung up the phone and shut down my computer. I knew what Charlie didn't say. There was no way to explain our relationship to someone who didn't endure what we did as children. But maybe he could convince Kathleen that I wasn't the cause of her problems.

I pushed the chair under the keyboard, knocking *Love's Savage Passion* from the edge of the desk where Sam Barlow left it. I grinned, remembering his face as he skimmed the pages. Just about every page in the book had some kind of purple prose. I wonder what he thought.

I started to put the book back on the shelf but on second thought I tucked it under my arm. A woman who reads romance novels never sleeps alone...

****

There was no ominous pickup truck idling at the curb when I opened the nursery the next morning. What I did find, though, was an unlocked back door and bags of fertilizer torn apart, the contents scattered on the concrete floor in the main building. A cloud of powdery haze greeted me when I flipped on the light switches. I backed away hastily when I saw that. We worked with masks and gloves around the bone and blood meal, common fertilizers, since mad cow disease made an appearance in the headlines. There was no way I was walking through a foggy room full of that stuff.

I suited up in disposable coveralls and masks, making sure to double-glove and double-bootie my shoes. I got out the broom, but the powder on the floor was slightly damp and almost impossible to sweep up. Whoever tossed it must have misted it after it was thrown about.

I finally settled for throwing a tarp over the smelly mess to let it dry and went on about my usual morning chores. I blocked off the area with a moveable metal display rack and tossed a tarp over it, too, just to make sure everyone knew the area was off limits.

"How could it happen?" Mary asked, bewildered, as we surveyed the scene when she came in several hours later.

"I have no idea." The residue was finally dry and I was sweeping the last of the powder into a pile. I pulled off my face mask. "The bags looked slashed, not torn," I said in a low voice.

"What?"

I led her to the corner where I stowed the bags under a metal display rack. "Look." I held up one of the nearly empty ten-pound bags.

"You're right." She looked at the clean cuts in the side of the white bag. The bags were heavy-duty paper, double-lined with crinkly plastic. It took a pair of sharp scissors or a sharp knife to get them open. I knew all about it since I tussled with those damn bags often enough.

Mary met my eyes. "Somebody did this on purpose," she whispered.

I nodded. "I think we need to talk to the police, Mary."

"We don't need this kind of trouble." She looked past me but Don and Bev, the other college workers, were both on the far side of the building stocking shelves with vases and pots. "I found rat poison in the kitchen area. It was sitting out in the open, not in a closed container."

"What? Who would put poison in there?"

"I don't know, but I get the feeling somebody has a grudge against us." Mary said this in a low voice, glancing around cautiously.

I stripped off my latex gloves and stuffed them into the trashcan next to the white disposable mask. "Why?"

"I don't know. I honestly don't. I can't think of anybody who might have a reason to wish us harm. But all of these pranks are more malicious than that."

"Where's Sam?"

Mary and I turned at the sound of the angry female voice. A woman came through the main door at the center of the shop and glared around the open space as though Sam Barlow was hiding just to annoy her.

"Crap, that's all we need," Mary muttered.

"Who is it?" I kicked off my plastic boot coverings then unzipped my disposable plastic clean-up suit. I clung to the wall as I started peeling it off.

"Sheila." Mary spat out the name like a bad taste in her mouth. She hurried across the open space to confront the other woman.

I examined Sam Barlow's ex-wife. She was about Mary's height, maybe five-eight or nine, and slender with thick, straight dark blonde hair in an attractive cut that framed her oval face. Her eyes were a remarkable pale blue and I wondered if they were contacts. Surely no one had such pale eyes? Even from a distance I saw her skin had a porcelain doll-like smoothness. I wondered if it was real or applied, then I mentally chastised myself. Just because I didn't have a deft hand with makeup didn't mean I should begrudge someone who did.

"Well, where is he? I told him I'd be here." Her voice was strident and loud, echoing in the big room with the high ceilings. She looked out of place in her chic dress and shoes that were so pointed they could open a vein if she nudged someone.

"Not everybody asks how high when you say

jump, Sheila."

Sam Barlow's calm, dispassionate voice came from behind me. I whirled to see him standing near the metal display racks I had pushed to one side when I started my cleanup. He must have been in the back storage room. He walked forward, eyeing the plastic suiting in my hands. "We need to talk about that," he said as he passed me.

"You're right. We do." I looked at the clock. "But I have to get to school now. I called Charlie and he said he could stop at three-thirty. Will that work for you?"

Sam nodded. "Thanks. I get the feeling I might need his help." Then he raised his voice slightly. "Let me give you my mobile phone number so you can give it to our lawyer, Mr. Whittington. We need to discuss those contract points." He made a show of pulling out a pad of paper from his flannel shirt pocket and jotting down a number, tearing it off and handing it to me just as his ex-wife approached.

"Sure," I said, playing along. "I'll have C.R. get in touch with you. I know he'll be happy to help you." I smiled at Sheila Barlow Peavey. "Excuse me."

She ignored me and snapped, "I have a funeral to plan, so this had better be good, Sam."

I beat a retreat, going out to my Jeep. As I drove out of the parking lot I saw a bright red Mustang parked in front, which must have been Sheila Peavey's car. Nice wheels and expensive ones. My Jeep wheezed as we passed the other car, probably in envy at the sight.

I merged onto the county highway and drove to my last day of class. Next week I'd take my final exams then I'd be done with school and could embark on my new career. It was a great feeling. My college degree and my weight loss were the big accomplishments I had achieved since my layoff from Lerner Software three years earlier. My world was unfolding before me, ripe with possibilities. As though to mimic my mood, the sun shone brightly and the piles of snirt along the road—snow mixed with dirt—were melting away, much like my past life was melting behind me. For some inexplicable reason, I felt like I was on top of the world.

As always, I had lunch with the ELLs and we exchanged phone numbers and promises to meet in the summer and to stay in touch. Barb and Susan would be in exams with me next week, so we made plans to lunch on Tuesday after the final test.

I looked for Aaron, but we didn't share any Friday classes. He was supposed to be working at Barlow's in the afternoon so I resolved to talk to him as soon as I could. No matter what Donna said, I think it was more than youthful hormones that had him in such a tizzy. I wanted to check with him and make sure he was okay.

I did my last round of chores in the old greenhouse, where the crime scene tape was finally removed. At three o'clock I was back on the road, heading for Pickaway. Thinking about Aaron made me remember our previous talk about sexual safety and on impulse I veered into a drugstore parking lot and went inside.

I'd never purchased condoms in my life. In my naïve birth-control-pill youth they weren't used extensively and in later years the man provided them. And of course, in the last few years it just hadn't been an issue. Once I hit a certain age I was content to stop worrying about sex and let life take its course.

I surveyed the bewildering array and settled on a 'Sampler Pack' which seemed a practical approach. That way if one kind didn't work or didn't fit...Fit? I examined the package. Did one size fit all? Surely not. After all, men weren't 'one size fits all.' I grinned as I remembered the SPAM ads I kept

69

getting and Sam Barlow's comment about the man providing the equipment. His dark eyes had just a hint of mischief when he said it and his lips had twitched as though he was—

The clerk passing by the aisle smiled at me. "Need any help?"

I dropped the box into my hand-held plastic basket. "Nope. Found it." The diet food was next to the sex items, which I suppose made convoluted sense. I grabbed a box of my favorite Atkins breakfast bars and was on my way.

When I got to Barlow's I saw Charlie's indigo blue Jaguar XJ in the parking lot. He wasn't in sight so I parked my Jeep and went into the main building. Charlie was talking to Mary Hannon, who appeared stunned by this apparition of male perfection in front of her. He was, as always, breathtakingly handsome in his tailored dark gray suit, white shirt and conservative dark tie. He's been mistaken for George Clooney in the past and today the resemblance was especially striking because of the suit, which looked like something out of *Ocean's Eleven*. His dark hair was flecked with gray and neatly combed into place and his dark green eyes, fixed on Mary, were like a hint of springtime.

He smiled and came forward to meet me. "You're looking good, C.R.," he murmured as he brushed a kiss against my cheek.

"You're looking good yourself, C.R." This was a standing joke of ours. We shared the same initials—C.R.W.—and occasionally had mixed-up mail when we were married. I saw Sam Barlow coming into the shop from the back door. He paused to stare at us. "Watch it," I murmured. "It's the boss man. No smooching on the job."

Sam's face revealed nothing as I introduced them and he shook Charlie's hand. Comparing the two men was like comparing a mustang to a thoroughbred or a football player to a soccer player. Sam exuded strength and confidence while Charlie was quietly elegant but equally masculine. Their clothing made the contrast even more blatant. Sam's worn blue jeans and flannel shirt with rolled up sleeves emphasized his muscular build and solid bulk. Charlie's tailored suit highlighted his broad shoulders and long legs, correctly making him appear to be lean and trim.

It was like comparing apples and oranges. Both were yummy but with entirely different flavors. Then I blushed at the thought. It was probably the condoms in the sack I held that had my mind going in such an unusual direction. "I'll leave you three to talk over the business details," I said, lightly twirling my plastic sack. "I've got to get to work."

"Spoken like a valued employee," Mary said with a smile. She gestured Charlie to the tiny office in the northeast corner of the building.

"Actually, I was hoping Cassie could join us," Charlie said with an apologetic smile. "I took the liberty of doing a bit of research and what I found affects her, too."

I blinked in surprise. "Really?"

"It affects all employees, but it might have something to do with..." Charlie lowered his voice. "You said odd things occurred here in the past month or so, right?" I nodded. "I wonder if what I found has to do with those things."

"Let's see if it does." Sam's voice was neutral but I'm sure he was skeptical. I could see it in his dark brown eyes.

We all walked through the store, Mary pausing to give directions to Bev who was manning the retail area. I glimpsed Aaron in the greenhouse as we passed the door and waved. He smiled briefly when he saw me.

I went into the little ten-by-ten office space and

Sam closed the door behind us. Charlie and I took the two wooden chairs in front of the battered oak desk where Mary sat. Sam leaned against the wall near the door and watched us, his eyes flickering from Charlie to me then to Mary, then back to me and Charlie again.

Charlie pulled a small leather-bound notepad from his suit pocket and opened it. "I checked the lease agreement your father signed with Mrs. Peavey," he said, flipping through the pages in the notebook.

"How did you see the lease agreement?" Sam asked, frowning.

"The agreement is public record," Charlie replied without looking up. "Because it involved deeded land and the city has zoning rights, it was filed at the courthouse and with the city. Here it is." He tilted the pad to get better light and I saw his angular, upright handwriting. "You really don't have a problem," he said, smiling at Mary Hannon. He glanced at Sam, whose frown deepened.

"I think you must be wrong. I talked to Sheila this morning and she swore she would never sell the land to us." Sam's voice was harsh. I could only imagine how those words must have stung coming from the woman he once loved. Or maybe she was the woman he still loved.

Charlie shrugged. "Doesn't matter. You don't need her to sell it to you."

"What?" Both Sam and Mary spoke at once.

"That doesn't make any sense, Charlie," I said. "She could sell the land out from under them. A friend at school said that a developer was anxious to buy this spot."

Charlie put a hand on my neck and gave me a little shake. "Hold on, motor mouth. I've got your explanation right here." He released me and held up his notepad. "She can't sell the land to Mr. Barlow or anyone as long as Barlow's Nursery continues in operation. Her father owned the land before he willed it to his daughter. It was a stipulation of the original agreement between her father and your father." Charlie smiled at Mary and Sam, but his smile faltered when he saw Sam's suspicious look.

"So as long as we stay in business, she can't sell it?" Sam asked.

Charlie nodded.

"So why does it affect me?" I asked. "You said it affects all employees and something about the odd..." My voice trailed off as I realized the implications of what he was saying. "You think somebody is trying to put us out of business?"

Charlie nodded. "And I just hope it doesn't escalate."

Chapter 7

"The truck," Sam said.

"What truck?" Mary and Charlie asked.

"You're not opening the store anymore early in the morning," Sam stated. "I'll do it."

"What truck?" Charlie demanded.

"There was a truck outside the other day when I opened," I said. "It was just sitting there with the motor running."

"He's right." Charlie looked at Sam. "He opens from now on. You shouldn't be out here alone."

I didn't try to argue with him. When Charlie got into his mother hen mode, there was no dissuading him. "You have to open the Roseville store," I said to Sam. "You can't do both stores."

"Stuart can do Roseville. I live a couple of miles from here." I started to speak but Sam just narrowed his eyes and said, "You can come in early, but not alone. I'm doing it. Whoever vandalized the place last night might still have been here when you opened the building."

"I was thinking about that today," I said.

"What vandalism? What's been happening? You told me about some dead birds and the water being left on and freezing." Charlie looked from me to Sam. "What else has happened?"

I put a calming hand on Charlie's arm. "I'll tell you later. Sam's right. I'll meet him here and we'll open together." I looked at Sam. "I was thinking about the spill this morning. When I came in the gate was locked but the building wasn't. So I started to think—what if somebody stayed in the building last night after closing? They could do the damage then leave. They could climb over the gate on the side or out through the front gate on the highway." The gate on the county highway was lower than the one on the side of the property and was meant more to keep cars from turning in than keeping vandals out.

"You think it's an employee," Sam stated flatly.

"But why?" Mary asked. She looked bewildered, her plain face scrunched up in thought. "We treat our people okay. Why would someone want to hurt us?"

I nodded to the notebook still in Charlie's hand. "To put you out of business?"

"A few dead birds? Some spilled pesticide?" Sam shrugged. "No big deal."

I considered how to phrase what I wanted to say. "It might be a big deal if an employee decided to sue because of injury." I cleared my throat slightly. "How financially stable are you? I know many nurseries overextend in the spring to stock the business and oftentimes have to rob Peter to pay Paul to stay afloat until summer money comes in." I avoided looking at Mary, instead glancing at Charlie. "I learned that in class. We had to take a business financials course."

"Makes sense." Charlie looked around the shabby room with the banged-up furniture and dingy walls. "You have a variable business dependent on client good will and reputation as much as anything. If something happens to damage the trust with your customers, it could hurt you."

"I can't think of any employee who would want to hurt us, though," Mary said.

"It's something to consider," Sam said thoughtfully. He pulled a manila folder off the desk. "This is the information I got from Sheila this morning. I tried to read it but it's written in Lawyer Speak and I can't figure it out."

Charlie took the folder and leafed through the documents inside. "Let me review this and get back to you." He pulled out his Blackberry, which wasn't black but indigo blue, matching his car. He consulted it, his green eyes flickering from one entry to another. "I'm a bit booked for the weekend, but I'll try to review it by Monday."

"How much is all this going to cost?" Sam asked, exchanging a worried look with Mary.

Charlie tucked his gadget back into his pocket along with his notebook. "We'll work something out. I'll give you the family rate."

I snorted. "Just don't charge them what you billed John."

Charlie laughed. "You're more family than he is. Any friend of Cassie's..." He stood and smiled reassuringly at Mary. "I think you'll be okay."

"As long as we stay in business." She blew out a long sigh. "Thanks, I appreciate your help. Both of you."

I followed Sam out of the room, my condom bag in hand. As we got to the front door, the bag bumped against the checkout counter and sagged open. Sam raised an eyebrow when the contents were displayed. "Planning on a little fun in the potting shed?" he asked.

"They're not for me," I assured him. "They're for—" Then I shut up. I couldn't reveal what Aaron told me in confidence. "Younger people are

76

embarrassed about buying them so I'm just helping out a friend."

He smiled slowly, his dark eyes mischievous. "Younger friend, hmm? Older woman younger man thing?"

"Oh for heaven's sake, I don't rob the cradle." I gestured with the bag to the door. "Come on, Charlie, I'll walk out with you. I'll be right back," I told Mary as Charlie and I left the building.

"They seem like nice people," Charlie commented as we sauntered to his Jag.

"They are. I hope they make it." I glanced back at the door where Sam was watching us. "I had access to some of their financial data when I set up a test program for them. Money is pretty tight."

Charlie leaned against the Jag and crossed his arms on his chest. "So I gathered. I'm assuming his divorce from his ex wasn't as amiable as ours?"

I followed his gaze and saw Sam disappear back into the building. "I don't think so. I'm sure this property is worth a bucket of money. Sheila Peavey would probably love to see it sold."

"I'll see if I can put a monkey wrench in her plans." He straightened and opened the car door. "He's interested in you."

"Huh?"

Charlie nodded toward the building. "Sam Barlow." He glanced down at the plastic bag I still held. "You might need those if you play your cards right."

"Not," I said flatly.

"Yep. I recognize the signs. I think he's interested in you and I don't mean employer-employee," Charlie said. "He's got his eye on you, girlfriend."

"Seriously?"

"Trust me. He's watching you."

I nudged Charlie. "Then maybe I might get a

chance to try out my new bod. I haven't had any action since I lost weight." Then I grinned. "Hell, I didn't have any action when I gained the weight, either, who am I kidding?"

"You were beautiful even when you were overweight," he said loyally.

"Thanks, Charlie, you're a friend. But you and I both know I looked like shit." I ran my hand through my newly shortened hair. "I'm a new woman."

He kissed me quickly then got into his Jag. "I loved the old woman as much as the new woman. I'll pick you up at noon tomorrow for the funeral."

I considered what he said as I went into the building. I was so out of the habit in the Love Department that I wasn't sure whether to believe Charlie or not. Luckily I didn't see Sam, otherwise I would have blushed like an idiot and made a fool of myself. I went to my locker and tucked away my gear, including the shopping bag, and pulled out my work jacket and gloves. I had pansies to water and fertilizer to apply. Any thoughts of Love—or sex— could wait.

I didn't see Aaron until I was well into my three hour shift. He was talking with Bev and Don in the employee break room. Like the other day, I was struck by how tired he looked. Dark circles rimmed his eyes and he jumped when I entered the room, like I startled him out of a year's growth.

"How's it going, guys?" I asked.

"Good." Bev put down the newspaper she was scanning. "So what do you think about the big scandal?"

"Hmm?" I headed for the coffee, safely stored in thermoses. Mary had hired a cleaning crew who came in and scrubbed the area until it shone. All food items were now stored in tins and the mugs were in a big plastic tub where they stayed until being put into the dishwasher at night. It was probably the cleanest break room I'd ever seen and certainly the cleanest I'd ever seen in a garden center. "What scandal?" I glanced down at the headline and wrinkled my nose. "Oh. That one."

Don laughed. "Yeah, that one. I don't get it." He was an out-going, personable twenty-something who looked more like a linebacker than a gardener. I was happy for his bulk, though, when it came time for heavy lifting around the place. I could always count on Don for hefting. "I don't care what anybody says, if I was a fifteen-year-old boy I wouldn't want to be hit on by my schoolteacher."

"And if I was fifteen years older than someone, I probably wouldn't want to hit on them." I glanced at Aaron, who stared at the newspaper with a fascinated look in his bright blue eyes. "It would be like me hitting on one of you guys or your older brothers." I shook my head. "You're nice guys but not romance material, you know?"

"Oh, I'm hurt." Don put his hand over his heart. "I was hoping for a little Mrs. Robinson action."

"Not with me." I got my mug out of the tub and poured some coffee, leaning against the counter to regard Aaron, skimming the news story. "What do you think about it?"

His head snapped up. "What? This?"

I nodded.

"I don't know..." He touched the picture in front of him. "She's good looking."

"Come on," Don said in dismissal. "She's almost thirty and he's like fifteen. Yuck."

"Maybe she was lonely," he said, his eyes sad.

"You're too charitable," I said. *And naïve,* I thought but didn't say. I saw Don start to make a joke and I changed the subject to spare Aaron further embarrassment. "When are your finals?"

"What? Oh, I've got most of them on Monday and Tuesday. That reminds me. I was talking to Ed.

He thinks we should go to the funeral."

My thoughts went immediately to the funeral I was attending on Saturday then I realized Aaron wouldn't know about that one. "What funeral?"

"Dr. Peavey's funeral. He thought we could represent the students and the school—you know, because we're officers in the Horticulture club."

"Oh, please," Bev said. "Like anybody will notice."

I thought of what Charlie told me about the grants. Somebody *might* notice. Perhaps we could make an impression on Peavey's business partners. If we did, they might continue the grant he applied for. The school could use the money. "When is it?" I asked.

"Tuesday afternoon, late in the day. I don't think they've released the body yet."

"Really?"

"The guy was murdered," Don pointed out. "They're probably cutting him up and examining all the pieces."

"And on such a happy note, I'm going back to work," Bev said with a laugh.

I laughed, too, but stopped when I saw the sick look on poor Aaron's face. I suppose it *was* a grim joke. "My finals are on Monday and Tuesday but they wrap up by noon. I was taking the rest of the week off before starting work full-time."

"I suppose you don't want to go to the funeral, then," he said despondently.

I hesitated then said, "Sure, I can go after my exams. I don't have anything planned for the rest of the day." I was just going to unpack some boxes and hang pictures and start working in my yard and...oh well. When I saw the thankful look on Aaron's face, I knew I made the right decision. "Do you want to meet at the school and we can drive together?"

He nodded. "I think if we met at two it would

80

give us plenty of time."

I calculated drive times and classes in my head and nodded. "I'll wear my funeral duds to class. Barb, Susan and I were going to lunch after our exams. I'll hang out and wait for you."

"Great. I didn't want to go alone." Aaron went to the lockers and twirled the combination lock on his.

"No problem." I watched Don, trying to mentally will him out of the room, but he stayed put, reading the newspaper and sipping a cup of coffee. My chance to discreetly hand over the condoms was fast disappearing.

"Don? Aaron?" Sam Barlow leaned into the doorway. "I need your help out here." His eyes met mine. "I need some muscle."

I held up my arm and made a fist, flexing my biceps as much as I could. "My girly muscles won't do?"

He raised an eyebrow. "Not for this. I need boy muscles." He moved away from the doorframe as Don joined him.

"Did you want to talk about that computer stuff?" I asked.

"Yeah. Let me finish this then I'll meet you in the office. Mary said she installed the sample software like you said."

Aaron closed his locker and hurried past me. "Thanks for going with me on Tuesday," he said in a low voice.

"No problem. I'll meet you there in a few minutes, okay?" I said to Sam.

He nodded and disappeared, helpers in tow. I tiptoed to the lockers and tested the handle of Aaron's locker. As I suspected, it closed but didn't latch. These old lockers needed jiggling to work. I pulled it open then opened my locker and transferred the condom bag to Aaron's, pulling out my breakfast bars as I did so.

I stopped and thought about it. How would it look if I put an entire box of condoms in there? Then I remembered Charlie's crack about me needing some of the condoms for my own use. I suppose it wouldn't hurt to be prepared, just in case. I looked around furtively but I was alone. I ripped open the box and saw four smaller boxes inside, each presumably holding a selection of the four types of condoms. I didn't bother to read the advertising, but I pulled out two of the inner boxes and stuffed them into the sack, jamming it into Aaron's locker. The other boxes I put back in my locker.

I almost fumbled the job and some papers spilled out of a folder at the bottom of Aaron's locker before I managed to tidy them and push them back inside. As I did, I saw the contents. I closed the door carefully, my mind in a whirl.

Why did Aaron have a manila folder full of press clippings about Michael Peavey? There were seven or eight articles, most with pictures of Peavey but some with Peavey and his wife or Peavey and another man. What did Aaron care about Mike Peavey and his doings?

I got my notebook labeled *Barlow Software Program* and left the break room, picking up my coffee mug on the way. I was almost to the office when I remembered. Mike Peavey and Aaron's father worked together. I knocked on the office door but no one was inside. The desktop computer was turned on with a sticky note on the chunky monitor screen: *Cassie: go ahead and use this, I have the software loaded. Mary.*

I put down my coffee mug and sat at the keyboard. A few keystrokes brought me search results on Min-Gen Technologies. I scanned the web site as I sipped my coffee. As I guessed, it was a botanical research firm with cultivation as their main specialty with a few genetic projects in the works. Michael Peavey was listed as the lead scientist and Joseph Swenson's name was listed as a primary researcher. Odd. They didn't update it yet to indicate Peavey was dead and Swenson wasn't there anymore. I suppose it would be poor advertising for investors to know your head honcho was poisoned in a greenhouse.

I opened a new window on the computer screen and accessed my email provider, intending to send Charlie a message about Min-Gen so he could find out their stock status. As always, the SPAM subject headers caught my attention.

Take MegaDik and be a man!

Men can experience multiple orgasms, too!

"Well, duh," I muttered. "Given the right incentive, I know they can." I deleted the noxious advertisements and quickly typed a note to Charlie, asking him to find out the status of Min-Gen stock. I clicked 'send' when I saw another email in my queue. I sighed.

Don't try to deny it, Cassie. Charlie is still in love with you and it's because of you he can't have a relationship with anyone else. Why don't you let him go? You've been divorced for almost thirty years but—

I didn't bother reading any more. I forwarded the email to Charlie with a note: *Charlie, you need to deal with this.*

As I sent it another SPAM popped up in the queue. "Is your penis size too small? Promote your soldier of love." I snorted with laughter as I read the foolish email out loud.

"Soldier of love? Really? What do I have to do to get a promotion?" a husky voice asked from the doorway.

I spun the chair so fast I nearly shot into space. Sam was leaned against the doorframe, grinning at me.

Chapter 8

My face got hot and I started to stammer a reply. Then to my surprise, Sam's face got red, too. "I'm sorry," he said. "That could be viewed as sexual harassment and it's not how I meant it."

His immediate apology startled me. I used his embarrassment to cover my flustered surprise. "I was out of line, too. I shouldn't be reading email on the job." I tore my eyes away from his and back to my computer screen. "Let's just forget it." I closed my email icon.

He came into the room to stand behind me. I looked over my shoulder and was eye-to-belt buckle with him. I snapped my head around to the front again, my ears flaming with color. "Can you see okay?" I asked, clicking the icon for the software.

"Yeah. Fine."

He was so close I felt his body warmth. Or maybe it was wishful thinking.

"I'm kind of out of practice," he said in a low voice.

"With computers? I tried to set this program up so it would be really easy to use. You can see—"

"With women."

84

I gaped at the computer screen, finally managing a squeaky, "Oh." Then I cleared my throat and said, "I guess I'm out of practice, too. With men."

"How long have you been divorced?"

I clicked a menu option and the main entry screen popped open on the computer monitor in front of me. "Almost thirty years. Charlie and I got married when we were in college. We were only married seven years."

"You're still friends with him."

I took a long breath. "Charlie and I grew up together. We had an...unusual childhood. I'll always be friends with Charlie."

There was silence behind me then he asked, "Are you still in love with him?"

I shook my head. "I love Charlie. But I was never in love with him." I craned my neck to look up into Sam's face. "And that's really all I care to discuss with you."

His dark eyes were puzzled but as soon as they met mine, I saw a mask of politeness fall into place. "Sure. I understand."

"No, you don't," I snapped, turning back to the program in front of us. "No one does. Charlie and I have given up trying to explain. You just have to trust me when I say he and I aren't involved in any way that affects my—I mean, in any way that would stop me—" I ground to a halt, not sure what I was blabbering.

"Sure. I get it." He leaned over me to point at something on the screen. "I think this column is in the wrong location. Our current checkout screen has it on the right side, not the left. It'll goof up the checkout clerks who have worked here before."

I pulled over my notebook and scrawled a line or two. "I've got it. What else?" I kept my voice coolly professional and so did he, pointing out a few items he thought should be changed. Twenty minutes later we finished. "I'll get those changes in tonight," I said. "We can go live next week if you want. I set it up so the data we collect can be funneled to the old system. That way if something goes wrong, we've got a backup plan. Do you want to implement the software at this store before we move on to the other one?"

Sam moved back around the desk and sat down in the guest chair I occupied earlier in the afternoon. "Is your ex-husband any good at what he does?"

The change of subject made me hesitate and think about my answer before saying, "Charlie's one of the best. Why?"

Sam propped his right ankle on his left knee and jiggled his foot. It reminded me of Aaron and his nervous tapping. "Sheila won't rest until she ruins me," he said flatly. "She'll do whatever it takes to put Barlow's out of business."

I leaned back in Mary's old oak desk chair and balanced carefully so I didn't tip too far. "Why do you say that?"

"Because it's the truth. Our parting wasn't as amiable as you and your ex. The minute Mike started to make a name for himself, she was gone." He looked around the cramped office. "Maybe I'm kidding myself. Maybe it wasn't Mike but..."

I held my breath, waiting for him to continue. When he didn't, I said, "It was a long time ago. Surely she's not carrying a grudge for anything that happened."

Sam shrugged. I didn't believe the supposed indifference in the action. His face was harsh and rigid, as though old memories were crowding him. "She's pretty damn upset right now about Mike's death. There's no telling what she'll do." His gaze shifted to the computer. "Let's go ahead and implement the program but I'm not sure we'll need it. If Sheila has her way, Barlow's will be gone from

Pickaway by the end of the season."

"There's the Roseville store," I said.

He nodded and stood. "Yep. And there are other locations where I could build here in Pickaway. I'm not sure I want to stay in the business, though, if it means a long court fight. But let's go ahead and figure on the best case scenario." He smiled wryly, the harsh lines around his mouth softening. "I guess it doesn't hurt to be an optimist." He started for the door then paused. "Thanks for the help."

I turned back to the computer to shut it down. "It's in my best interest to see the place succeed," I said lightly. "I like working here."

"Good." His voice was soft and caressing.

My head whipped around and I met his eyes. I smiled tentatively.

"I like to keep the employees happy," he said in a low voice. Then he turned and left the office, leaving me a bit overheated and immobile with surprise.

****

I was glad I had my garage door opener because a steady rain started to fall just as I left the landscape center. The night was cold, with temperatures only in the forties, but I was happy to have it be that warm. At least we had rain and not snow. Maybe spring would finally arrive after all.

By the time I got home I was eagerly anticipating to a bowl of chili and a relaxing night in front of the television. Alas, it wasn't to be. I just finished microwaving the chili extracted from my freezer when the phone rang. I didn't recognize the caller ID number so I let the answering machine pick up.

"Cassie, this is Kathleen Emerson. Charlie called me and told me you forwarded my email to him. You know what I said was true. You need to let Charlie go. He's still in love with you. How can I—

how can anybody—compete with that? It's time you two sat down and talked about your relationship. Charlie told me about what happened when you were kids. I understand why you're close, but you need to let him go." There was a crashing noise. I realized she'd slammed the phone down.

I stared at the answering machine in amazement. She sounded quiet, calm, and rational until the final crash, as though what she was suggesting was the simplest thing in the world to do. I reached for the phone then hesitated. Despite what Kathleen said, I knew the truth. Any supposed love Charlie still felt for me was mingled with pity and memory. If his relationship with Kathleen didn't succeed, it wasn't because of me.

I wandered into the dining nook, bowl of chili in hand and sat down. I automatically ate, Houdini winding around my ankles as I stared at the rain pounding down outside, deep in thought. No one in the Whittington family, father or children, had a happy marriage. Were we forever scarred by what happened when we were children? It was a sobering thought and one I didn't want to pursue.

I put the chili, half-eaten, into the sink and went into the Box Room, where I examined some boxes and decided to put them into storage. As I wrestled the boxes down to the basement I belatedly remembered my plan to get a dehumidifier for the storage room behind the furnace. They were on sale at the local big box hardware store but the sale ended today.

I went back upstairs and checked the weather. The rain was now a fine drizzle. The store was just a couple of miles away and if I hurried, I could get there and get back in time for a CSI rerun on cable. I patted Houdi on the head and was out the door in a few minutes.

I drove by Barlow's Nursery on the way. It was

hard to see much in the rain and fog, but I could tell the gates that faced out on the county highway were closed. Mary and Sam were in the main building when I left ninety minutes earlier, but now the lights were off and the place looked empty.

When I passed thirty minutes later on my way home, I saw a light on in the main building. At first I thought it was a reflection from the rain on the pavement but when I turned the corner onto Barlow Boulevard, the light didn't waver.

I turned around in the drive and went by again on the highway side, this time slower. There was definitely a light on in the main building. It flickered, so it was hard to tell but it looked like someone might be walking inside. I turned back onto Barlow Boulevard and parked the Jeep near the side gate, fumbling my cell phone out of my pocket.

When I moved into my townhouse I discovered my cell phone signal strength in this part of town was weak. I hadn't switched carriers yet but it was high on my Shit To Do list even though I seldom used the phone, mainly just for long distance and times like this, when I needed a phone and none was in sight.

I laboriously found Mary Hannon's home phone number in my cell phonebook and dialed it, but there was no answer. I started to call 911 then remembered Sam Barlow gave me his number earlier that day. I fished it out of my pocket and he answered on the first ring.

"Hey, this is Cassie Whittington. I was driving by the office and I see lights on in there. Is somebody inside tonight?"

"Where are you?"

"I'm on Barlow Boulevard, near the side gate. I drove by twice and there's a light inside. It looks like it's moving."

"Are you sure it's not just because of the rain?

That can create an optical illusion sometimes."

"I'm sure. I drove by again to check it from a different angle." I hesitated, remembering Mary's earlier concern about someone with a grudge. "Do you want me to call the police?"

Sam must have remembered it, too. "I'll be right there. I'm just a few blocks away. Don't go in."

No kidding I wouldn't go in. I closed the phone and put it back in my pocket, tapping my fingers on the steering wheel. What to do? Wait? Go? I peered at the main building but the tree lot was hiding most of my view. I was just getting ready to turn the Jeep around when a maroon SUV pulled up behind me and Sam Barlow got out, still dressed in the clothing he wore earlier at the store.

"Boy, you really were nearby," I said as I unrolled my window.

He leaned over to peer at me. "I was just getting home from the Roseville store. Where did you see the light?" I started to get out but he put a hand on the door, stopping me. "Just tell me. I'll check it."

His offer was tempting but I didn't relish the idea of sitting in my Jeep and waiting to see what happened. I described where I saw the light. "Should I call the police?"

Sam looked past me, to the building in the distance. "Let me check it first. Maybe Mary left the light on." He started around the front of my Jeep.

I hastily turned off the motor and got out.

"Stay there," he said, striding away into the damp night.

"I'm not staying there," I said, scrambling after him as he approached the gate. "The Pervert might get me."

"Then go home," he said, angling the combination lock so the security light overhead shone on it.

"I can't. You parked behind me."

He glanced back at our vehicles. "Damn. You're right." He hesitated as the lock sprang open in his hands. "I'll move it and—"

"No, you won't. Come on. Let's go inside." I started to push the gate open but he put a hand on my arm, pulling me back.

"Get your car and we'll drive in."

I hurried back to my Jeep and angled it through the gate. Sam got into the passenger side after closing the gate behind me. "Park in front," he directed. "Use the headlights to shine on the front door. I'll go in that way."

I did as he directed, parking so the front of the Jeep directly faced the main door. Sam hopped out and was at the door, his key ring in hand, before I even knew he was gone. The misty rain swirled through the headlights, giving the scene an out-of-focus, arty look, like some kind of film noir piece.

He quickly opened the door and pushed it wide, disappearing inside. When the interior lights came on, I turned off the motor and followed him. He was moving toward the office on the left where we all met earlier about the contract. The safe was there and it was where they kept money for opening in the morning in case we had customers before Mary could get to the bank. I started to follow him but I heard a scuffling sound from my right, in the far corner of the store near the employee break room. "Sam," I hissed. "Over there."

He looked back at me then at the employee area where I was gesturing. "What?"

"I heard something."

He stopped, obviously torn between following his instinct or mine. When I started toward the break room, he muttered something and hurried after me. I stopped outside the room and tested the doorknob cautiously.

"Wait," he breathed softly.

I stepped back as Sam moved by me, slipping into the room with barely a sound. I peeked around the doorframe after him. He walked back to the lockers, giving the area a quick look-over then he came back to me. "Where did you see the light?"

"Over there." I gestured to the front of the store, to the part that faced the county highway. "I thought I saw something or someone near the west checkout door."

Sam skirted the employee area and peered around the door into the restroom in the back west corner of the building. 'Restroom' was really a glorified term for a washing-up mudroom used by employees. The real bathrooms, used by the public and staff, were at the opposite end of the building.

Sam came out of the tiny room and looked at me, shrugging. "I'm not seeing anything." He started toward the office when the scuffling sound came again, this time almost directly behind him. The locked storage room between the mudroom and the employee lounge was where we wheeled display racks of our more expensive pottery and gardening tools. It was a tiny space, about ten foot square with an overhead light sharing a circuit with the light in the employee break room next door.

Sam extracted his keys and unlocked the door, pulling it open slowly before going inside. I hesitated just a minute then followed, not anxious to be left standing out in the open. The door to this room was tricky, with an over-enthusiastic hinge. It had a habit of slamming shut behind you if you weren't careful. I made sure it was forced well back on its hinges before I edged inside.

Shadows cast by the inadequate lighting made it hard to see anything clearly. I'm not claustrophobic but the crowded windowless room always gave me the feeling someone was looking over my shoulder, and often something was—a praying angel, a statue, a yard ornament, or a lawn flag. Flamingoes, smiling turtles, alert bunnies, and even a few pigs were all lined up, waiting for their chance to be put on display and taken to a good home. A garden bench with intricate wooden scrollwork on its back was pushed against the wall shared with the employee break room. The heirloom seed racks were near it, making it appear like the large bench was behind a fortress of vegetables, flowers, and herbs.

I edged into the room then turned, jumping back in surprise. A life-sized concrete St. Francis smiled gently at me, a plaster pigeon on his shoulder. St. Frank held a large shallow dish that looked suspiciously like a pizza tray, although it was made from polished steel shining dully in the meager light. "Damn saints," I muttered as my heart resumed beating normally.

"We've had Frank for so long we should just put him in the tree lot," Sam said, glancing at me. "I don't know why Mary bought him. Nobody's going to pay that kind of money for a yard ornament."

I twitched the price tag hanging off St. Frank's sleeve and whistled. "Wow. Three hundred bucks?" I patted Frank's arm. "No offense, but I don't think my birds care if you're out there or not, blessing them. As long as I get the seed out, they don't care about the carrier."

Sam bent over, inspecting something on the floor. "Pickaway isn't affluent enough. Now if it was the Minnetonka or Uptown neighborhood? Yeah, somebody there would pay a lot for Frank. But we don't get that kind of clientele here."

I inched around Sam, spying colorful packages among the concrete livestock on the farthest wall. "Oh, no," I muttered. "Look." I knelt by a display of overturned seeds, the packets scattered on the floor.

"Mice," he said in disgust. "They must have gotten in and knocked it over."

"It wasn't mice using a light and walking around earlier," I said, standing up. I started toward the door but this time I heard another door, somewhere in the distance. "Somebody's out there."

"Would you wait? Let me handle this." Sam started to push past me, his exasperation evident now in his brusque manner.

The lights went off. Inky darkness instantly enveloped us. I stumbled to one side, disoriented. "Hey!"

Sam pulled me to him, helping me find my balance. "Are you okay?" His face was very close to mine. I felt his warmth and his scent wafted near me, a faint pizza aroma mingled with a whiff of aftershave and warm flannel shirt.

"What happened?" I put my hands on his arms, gripping tightly. "Did the fuse blow?" I looked past him, but could barely see the outline of the doorway. "All the lights are out."

He twisted in my grasp but I kept hold, not sure where I was in the room. Was the seed rack nearby? What about Frank? With my luck I'd run right into the concrete saint and knock myself out. I took a cautious step toward Sam and he put his arm around me.

"Come on." He started to lead me toward the door, our bodies pressed close to each other. If I hadn't been so scared, I would have enjoyed it.

The door slammed shut in front of us.

Chapter 9

"Damn it," Sam snapped. He headed for the door, me in tow behind him, clinging to his shirt.

"What is it? Where's the door?" I heard the panic in my voice but I didn't care. I *was* panicked. Sam released me and I stopped, unsure of where I was in the windowless room. "Sam? Where are you?"

I heard a hollow rattling sound.

"Sam?"

"I'm here. The door's locked."

"What?" I took a step forward and ran into him, the solid expanse of his chest hard against my face. I put my hands on his shoulders. "What's going on?"

"I'm not sure."

"Is somebody out there? Did they lock us in?"

"Shh. Let me listen."

"Listen? To what? How come—"

His fingers touched my neck, sliding upward until he could cup my face in his hand. "Cassie," he whispered softly. "Don't worry. Just let me listen." His hand moved away, leaving my skin feeling surprisingly cold behind it.

I was so surprised by his touch I shut up. I strained to hear anything but couldn't concentrate because of my thudding heart and the nausea in my stomach. "What do you hear?" I finally whispered.

"I think the outside door closed."

"We're alone?" My voice rose slightly. I reached out, trying to feel the wall. What I felt was Sam's butt instead. "Oh. Sorry."

"No problem." He sounded amused.

I fumbled my cell phone out of my pocket. "Maybe I can call somebody," I muttered. I flipped it open and the light illuminated Sam, his hand on the doorknob. It was a sign how stygian dark it was that my cell phone seemed as bright as a nova.

"Call Mary," he said, rattling the knob again. "I'd rather not have the police out here if we can help it."

"But if somebody locked us in, the police should know." I stared down at my cell phone screen, trying to will the little 'connect' bars into activation. It didn't work. Only one short bar flickered to life then out again. "I can't get a signal. Try your phone." I walked slowly to the other side of the room, angling the phone away from me like a flashlight, praying for a signal. I alternately used it to guide me and peered at the screen, eyeing the bars hopefully.

I glanced back at Sam and saw a faint glowing light.

"The battery's low," he muttered. "I might have enough for one call."

"How low? When did you charge it last?"

"Hold on." Sam put the phone to his ear. "Mary, it's Sam. Cassie and I are at the store and we're locked in. Get over here as soon as you can. You might want to call the police, too, because I think someone..." He pulled the phone away and looked down at it. "No power. At least I got some of the message on her machine. She and Joe were going out tonight."

"Great," I snapped. "So we have to sit here and

wait for them to come home?" I strode to the door in the meager light from my phone, staring at the door then down at my display. The damn bars were still so low I could barely see them.

"I guess so," Sam said. The faint blue light from his phone flickered and died. "I lost my charger when I moved back here from Florida. I've been using the charger I keep in the truck and I keep forgetting to plug it in."

"Damn it. So how are we supposed to get out? Can we break down the door?" I pushed hard against it but it didn't budge.

"Whoa. Wait a minute." He pulled me back.

I struggled against his grip. "Let me go. We have to get out."

"Are you claustrophobic?" Sam's arm tightened around my shoulders and I felt the warmth of his body against mine.

I tried to draw away. "No, but I don't like being locked in the dark with somebody I barely know."

He immediately released me. "Sorry. I just figured if you were spooked..."

I took a long, steadying breath. "No, I'm sorry. It's not your fault. It's just that I have to—" I cast about for something that sounded plausible. I couldn't explain why I was feeling panic, but I was. "I have to sing tomorrow."

There was a long silence. "I beg your pardon?"

"I have to sing tomorrow. At a funeral. So I have to get out so I can sing."

"What time?"

"Huh?"

"What time is the funeral?"

"Oh. Charlie's picking me up at noon."

"I'll think we'll be out by then," Sam said dryly. "Why do you have to sing?"

"It's a family thing. I sing at weddings and funerals, usually with the other Whittingtons to accompany me."

"What are you singing?"

"*Amazing Grace* and a couple of other songs Grandy picked out."

"Grandy?"

"Charlie's grandmother. She sort of adopted me when I was little."

"So sing something," he said, his disembodied voice coming from a spot near my right hand.

"What?"

"Sing something. Sing what you're going to sing there. Don't you need to practice?"

"I can always practice but—"

"We're not going anywhere until Mary checks her phone messages. She and Joe were going to a movie, so they'll probably be back soon." I heard a creaking noise and I knew he was settling back on the bench. "Go ahead. Are you shy?"

"Hardly. I've been singing in front of crowds most of my life."

"So go ahead. Maybe it'll calm you down."

"I don't need to be calmed down."

"Really?"

I started to snap a reply then realized he was right. Singing always did calm me. "I haven't practiced this song much," I warned him.

"I promise to be gentle in my critique." His voice was again dry and humor-filled. I knew he had no idea what to expect. When I told people I sang, they expected someone with an average-to-good voice. What most people didn't know was I was classically trained for almost ten years and sang semi-professionally for almost twenty years.

"Thanks." I closed my eyes even though I didn't need to with the darkness of the light-less room surrounding me. It was a habit my voice instructor had drilled into me years ago, though, and it was part of my preparation ritual. I visualized the sheet music and heard the tune in my mind, mentally adjusting it so it was in the key I wanted. Then I straightened and let my arms fall to my sides, relaxing my shoulders and lifting my chin to face the invisible audience in front of me. I launched into *Oh, Had I Golden Thread,* a challenging song to sing a cappella.

When I finished, Sam was silent for a moment. "That was great."

I heard the sincerity in his voice. "Thanks. I haven't practiced it much."

"What else are you singing?"

"A Billie Holiday song—*I'll Be Seeing You.*"

"Go ahead. I'd like to hear it."

I hesitated. "It's better when Charlie accompanies me."

"Everything's better with Charlie, isn't it?"

I wasn't quite sure what I'd heard. "I'm sorry?"

"That's the way it sounds. Everything's better with Charlie."

"You don't understand." I started to pace but stopped when I realized I would probably trip over something. I made my way back to where I was before, reaching out tentatively. My fingers brushed against Sam's face and I jerked away. He put a hand on my arm and pulled gently. I ended up sitting down, very close to him.

I started to scoot to my right but he put a hand on my knee, stopping me. "What's to understand?" Sam murmured in a soft voice. "Charlie's handsome, he's rich, he drives a Jag, he wears nice clothes. Of course everything's better with Charlie."

I gestured impatiently, the movement sliding me even closer to him. "None of that matters. It's not about the money." I knew I sounded stupid, but it was true. "It's about the past."

When I didn't continue he said, "Go ahead and tell me. I bet I'll understand."

I shook my head then realized he couldn't see me. "It's a long story."

"Like I said, we're not going anywhere." He leaned closer. "Cassie, please. I'd like to know more about you." When I hesitated, he put an arm around my shoulders and pressed me against him. "Tell me."

I stiffened but he didn't let me go. I finally relaxed, feeling the reassuring thump of his heart and the slight rumble of his stomach as he digested whatever he ate that night. The prosaic sound made me smile even as I sorted my jumbled thoughts. I realized I wanted to tell him. I was tired of defending my friendship with Charlie to him and to others. I probably couldn't make him understand but I might feel better for trying. "It happened when we were children," I said slowly.

"What happened?" I couldn't see his face, but I heard the sympathy in his voice.

"My father physically and sexually abused my mother. Back then...this was the Sixties. People didn't talk about it. Women just put up with it. But my mother..." I swallowed the bitterness I always felt whenever I remembered. "My father hit me and my mother was afraid he might...do something to me."

Sam's hand tightened around me. I felt fingers squeeze my upper arm. "Did he assault you?" he whispered.

"No, but Mom was afraid he would. She took me and we ran away." I paused, a chaos of images in my brain. "There were just a couple of women's shelters back then. My mother ran away from him and Gloria Whittington, Charlie's mother, helped her. Gloria volunteered at the shelter and she was trying to raise money to get more shelters built. Gloria was passionate about women's rights and the women's movement. She took my mother and me in, gave us a place to stay at their house. That's how Gloria was."

I remembered the beautiful woman who seemed like a vision to me when I was a child. She was the guardian angel who took us out of the grungy, dismal shelter and into her bright, beautiful home on pristine Lake Minnetonka in the swanky suburbs of the Twin Cities.

"That was generous of her."

"Gloria didn't think the way other people did. It was the right thing to do so she did it. There was never a question about whether it was the socially acceptable thing to do. Gloria had a firm sense of morality and she followed it. Having us stay with her worked out well for all of us. Mom had a background in education and Gloria was looking for a nanny. It was a win-win situation for everybody. We were with the family for almost six months. Everything was fine until my father found us."

"How old were you?" Sam prompted. His hand took mine and I clung to him, feeling the old trembling begin.

"Charlie was ten. I was eight. The Whittington twins, John and Becky, they were five. Olivia, Charlie's little sister, was just a baby. The family has a house on Lake Minnetonka, a big old place with lots of shoreline. It's one of the oldest estates on the lake. You've probably seen pictures of it in books. It happened in the summertime. We were at the lake, playing on the beach near the boat dock. Gloria and my mother were there. Charlie's dad was at the house. I could see him in his study. It overlooked the lawn and the beach. He liked to work in his office and watch us out on the beach. Sometimes he came out and joined us."

Sam squeezed my fingers when I stopped. "Tell me," he whispered.

"You probably read about it." It still hurt to talk about it. Even after all this time, my throat closed up as I remembered. I struggled onward. "This was before security systems and security cameras." I laughed bitterly. "This was before people worried about crap like stalkers and crazy families and psychopaths."

Sam squeezed my hand again. I swallowed hard. "My father walked around the side of the house with a shotgun. Charlie saw him first. He grabbed me and the twins then pushed us to the ground before he went after my father. I heard the shots but I didn't see it. When I looked up, my mother was struggling with my father for the gun. Charlie was lying half-in, half-out of the water at the shoreline with blood on his face. He wasn't moving. Baby Olivia was lying on the ground, near Gloria, crying and waving her arms. Charlie's mother had turned so the shotgun blast took her in the back. She protected Olivia." My voice shook and I took a long, ragged breath.

"I remember," Sam whispered. "The Charity Murder. I remember people talking about it. I wasn't old enough to really understand."

I nodded even though he couldn't see me in the dark. "That's what they called it because Gloria's charity killed her. Charlie had jumped my father, but he kicked Charlie in the face. Charlie went down in the water. I knew he'd drown so I ran to him and tried to drag him out. Then I heard another shot." I closed my eyes but the image remained, burned on my memory. "My father pushed my mother away and aimed the shotgun at her. But Charlie's father came out of the house with a hunting rifle. He shot my father. I remember my father's face, exploding into little bits of blood. He landed right beside me. I was in the lake, in the shallows, and my father fell there. The water turned red." I took a gulping breath. "Charlie grabbed me and held me. He tried to shield me but it was too late. I saw it." Tears rolled unheeded down my cheeks. "Now do you know why I love Charlie?"

Sam put his arms around me and I burrowed my head against his shoulder. "Yes," he whispered. "Now I know."

"Charlie's dad, C.R. the Second, he let us stay."

"What? You stayed there, with the family? But..." Sam's voice trailed off as the implications of what I was saying sunk in.

"C.R. needed somebody to take care of the kids and my mother...I suppose she was guilty or felt she owed him. I think they were both in such shock they didn't know what to do. He hired Mom as the nanny and she raised all of us the kids. I was raised in the house alongside the Whittington children. I was seventeen when she died. Charlie and I were married three years later." I shook my head, smelling Sam's warm, comforting scent. "Do you see now why I have such ties to Charlie and his family?"

"I do." Sam's voice was gentle and understanding. "But Cassie—you've paid your penance."

I drew back slowly. "It's not like that."

"Of course it is."

His self-assurance made my temper flare immediately. "You don't know anything about it. I've known Charlie all my life. We're good friends."

"He's still in love with you."

"Oh, bullshit." I pushed away from Sam and stood. "You've seen him, what—once? And based on seeing him once, you know he's in love with me? That's crap."

"I know the symptoms," Sam said, his voice quiet but assured. "Believe me, I know what it looks like. If you don't love him, you should cut him loose."

"You and Kathleen should get together and compare notes," I snapped.

"Kathleen?"

"Charlie's girlfriend. She said something similar."

"Maybe she's right." I heard him stand then felt him very near to me. "You need to decide if you're ready to move on, Cassie."

"I have moved on. Why does everyone think it's insane because Charlie and I are friends?" I started to turn away but Sam put a hand on my forearm, keeping me close even when I twisted in his grip. "Stop it. You have no right to say anything about me and Charlie."

He released me. "I know I have no right. But I need to know how you feel, Cassie."

"Feel about what?"

"About him." His voice was harsh and demanding.

"I told you. We're friends."

"Are you sure it's just friendship?" He moved even closer, his chest pressing against me. Then his arms went around me and I sensed his face close to mine.

"It's none of your business." I leaned back.

"It's my business if I can't get involved with you," he whispered. His lips touched mine in the dark. I was so startled I pulled away but he put a hand on the back of my head and kept me near him. "Cassie?" he murmured.

"I don't know—I—why—?" I lifted my head, bringing my lips back to his. "Sam?"

His lips were gentle against mine, tentatively moving. Tentative, that is, until I put my arms around him. Then we were suddenly in a rough embrace, gripping each other with an intensity that floored me. It was years since I felt such overwhelming passion, but I hadn't forgotten how it felt: hot, excited, nervous, anticipatory, anxious. I ran my hands over his back, feeling the hard muscles and the warmth of him. I couldn't believe I ever thought he was not a big man. Sam Barlow was big, broad-shouldered and...I wiggled slightly. Yep.

He definitely didn't need to pay attention to those Viagra emails.

"This isn't right," I said as I tore my lips away from his. "I work for you."

"You work for Mary." He kissed his way down the side of my face, his breath tickling and warm on my neck.

"But you're the owner." I was breathless with anticipation. The dark added an erotic touch to everything he did. I didn't know where his hand would be next or where his lips would move. I shivered with anticipation.

"I'm a co-owner. Trust me. It's not a problem." His right hand slipped under my jacket and cupped my breast. "I'll manage to restrain my favoritism." His breath tickled my ear as he whispered, "We have some time until Mary gets here. Care to get acquainted?"

"Here?" My voice squeaked with disbelief. "In the storage room?"

"Hmm. You're right. It's not very comfortable." He suddenly moved, pulling me to him. I gave a little shriek as I came down on his lap. "Let's see what we can do."

"Sam, we shouldn't do this. I work for you." I shivered as he slipped a hand under my sweater and his cold fingers touched my breast. "I shouldn't...oh." I leaned back slightly.

"You shouldn't what?" He kissed me again, our lips meeting hungrily.

"I shouldn't be thinking what I'm thinking," I said when we finally broke apart.

"And what are you thinking?" He pinched my nipple gently and I moaned.

"About getting naked," I admitted.

He laughed softly. "Good. I'm thinking the same thing."

"Sam?"

We heard Mary's voice as the lights came on, flooding us with a bright glare. I stared at him, wide-eyed.

"Oops," he whispered.

I slid off his lap, my face hot with color. "Good thing we didn't act on that thought," I muttered as I tugged down my sweater.

"It might have been awkward." He stood and kissed me quickly. "But keep it as an option, okay?" Then he turned to the doorway. "In here, Mary!"

I ran a hand through my hair, not sure what to say to this stranger who made me moan just moments before. He smiled at me, but his dark eyes were serious and worried. "Think about it, okay?"

"What?"

"What I said about Charlie. I don't want to get involved with someone who isn't really free, you know?"

"I'm available," I said.

He shook his head. "Think about it. You and Charlie need to talk." Then he turned to meet Mary Hannon, who was opening the locked door.

Chapter 10

The police arrived with Mary, who had called them before she left home to find us. In the bustle of their arrival, Sam and I were separated. I stammered out an explanation of how I came to be there, my story enhanced by Sam giving his brief account of my phone call and what happened when we got into the store.

"At least we went to the early movie," Mary said in commiseration as she and I stood near the office and watched Sam examine the safe, a uniformed police officer by his side. "Otherwise you and Sam would have been stuck here a lot longer."

I was glad my face was in shadow so she couldn't see how red I got. Who knows what might have happened if I was 'stuck' any longer with Sam Barlow? Good heavens, she might have walked in on us, naked and—

"You may as well go on home now," she said. "Sam and I can deal with this. No need for you to waste any more of your Friday night." She gave me a comforting pat on the arm.

Sam glanced at me over his shoulder and our eyes met. "Thanks," he said.

107

I nodded, not sure what to say.

"I unlocked the front gate," Mary said. "You can go out that way since Sam's truck is still blocking the side gate."

"Okay." I started toward the front door. I looked back once. Sam was still watching me, his face impassive. Then the police officer said something to him and he turned, going to the desk and the computer sitting there.

I went out to my Jeep, moving like a robot with staccato jerks as I tried to hide my astonishment that I had almost leapt into bed—or onto a garden bench—with a total stranger. I was trembling so badly I could barely fit the key into the ignition and when I started the Jeep, I almost stalled it, trying to back away from the storefront.

What the hell just happened? Did Sam Barlow put a spell on me?

By the time I got home, I had my brain somewhat under control. It was my hormones, I decided. I was starting the Change and my hormones were in an uproar. All those books I read about menopause didn't mention the rampant horniness or stray lustful thoughts I got when I saw an attractive man. I vowed to be more on my guard in the future. Heaven only knew what might happen if I was caught up in the throes of hormone lust and the wrong guy was at hand. I didn't even want to think about it.

I hooked up my new dehumidifier then showered and got into bed after popping in an old Miami Vice DVD on the miniscule TV that occupied the top of my dresser. I always watched MV in the wintertime just to remind myself of what warmth was like. I settled back with a happy sigh to watch Crockett and Tubbs fight bad guys. About halfway through the first episode, my phone rang. It was Sam.

"Cassie? I wanted to make sure you got home okay."

"Sure, I'm fine." I muted the sound of a gun battle in progress and snuggled into my bed, Houdini draped on my thigh and purring loudly. "Is everything okay?"

"Yeah. Nothing was missing or out of place that Mary or I could find. The police think you and I might have scared the guy away."

"Good. I'm glad nothing's wrong."

He hesitated. "Listen—I was wondering—can I come over?"

I said the first thing that popped into my head. "I'm in bed."

He laughed. "That works for me."

Damn. Wrong thing to say if I wanted to stave him off. "I'm not sure, Sam."

"Not sure? About what?" Before I could answer, he continued. "I'd like to see you, Cassie. How about tomorrow?"

I had a legitimate excuse this time. "I might be busy. There's the funeral I have to go to. I have to sing, remember?"

"How about Sunday?"

Now it was my turn to hesitate. "I meant what I said. I'm not sure it's right for me to go out with the boss."

"Just for coffee. We can talk about it."

I watched Sonny Crockett on my little TV as he drove his fancy sports car at breakneck speeds through the magically empty streets of Miami. I was feeling a bit adrenalized myself, a sympathetic partner to Detective Crockett. "Okay, maybe in the morning on Sunday. I have to study in the afternoon."

"I'll help." His voice was low and husky. I shivered at the sound.

"Why don't you give me a call tomorrow night

and we'll set a time?"

"Okay. Good night, Cassie. Sleep tight."

"Good night, Sam." I hung up the phone slowly and turned up the sound on the TV just in time to hear Crockett say, 'Damn it, what's going on?'

I knew exactly how he felt.

****

The next morning, I managed to tuck in a few hours of studying between unpacking then I dressed in my all-purpose navy slacks with navy and white sweater set. As I pulled on my 'marrying-and-burying clothes,' I eyed my pesticide books, still strewn on my bed from the night before when I fell asleep with them next to me as I watched TV.

There were any number of chemicals that might have killed Michael Peavey but most of the ones I was studying were immediately toxic, not delayed-effect poisons. I couldn't think of any horticultural chemical that took days to kill. Several might cause serious illness over time, but death? Usually death occurred within minutes, or hours at the most.

On impulse I went into the den and was just starting a web search when Charlie's blue Jaguar XJ pulled into my driveway. I set up a Google search then logged off as Charlie honked once. I grabbed my coat and purse and was out the door before another honk ensued.

"Hey, C.R.," Charlie said as I pulled open the door and slid onto the dove-gray leather seats. "You're looking good, girlfriend."

I leaned over for his kiss then buckled up as he pulled out of the driveway. Charlie appeared tired, with dark circles under his eyes. "You're looking good yourself, C.R."

"Ready to deal with the mob?" he asked as we left my middle-class subdivision and headed north toward the pricier enclaves of Minnetonka.

"As ready as I can ever be with your family." I

leaned back, enjoying the soft seats, warm sunlight and the quiet strength of the expensive vehicle. The day was sunny and the air had a humid smell, full of moist earth and future possibilities. "This is such a nice car."

Charlie grinned at me. "You've said that about every Jag I've ever owned."

"And I meant it."

"And I meant what I said. I'll sell you one of my used ones, just say the word." He winked at me. "I'll even give you a good deal."

I laughed. "I can't afford the insurance, Charlie. I'll keep the Wrangler until it coughs its death throes on the highway, then I'll buy another Jeep.

He glanced at me as we merged onto the northbound freeway. "I wish you'd let me help you, Cassie."

"I'm doing fine," I assured him. "Believe me, if push ever came to shove, I'd take your money fast enough. But so far, so good." That wasn't strictly true, of course. I didn't have much of an emergency fund any more, and my retirement savings were meager, but true retirement was a few years away and I had time to fatten up that account.

The big car slid noiselessly through traffic with only a hum of engine and J. J. Cale on the CD player to indicate it was moving. I thought of my Jeep and its rattles, whistles, and belches. "I hate to tell you this, Charlie, but Kathleen called me last night."

His hands tightened on the leather-covered steering wheel. "Damn it, I told her to back off. What did she say?"

"I didn't pick up the phone. She said something about how you were still in love with me and I needed to turn you loose." I looked away from him, embarrassed. "The same old shit. Nobody seems to understand how we can be friends. Sam Barlow gave me crap about it last night, too." I shook my head in

"Last night? Did you have a hot date?" His tone was teasing but I heard an undercurrent of real curiosity.

I told him about the previous evening's activities, leaving out the hot kisses on the wooden bench. "Sam said they didn't find anything wrong, so I suppose it was just vandalism." I finished recounting my adventure as we skirted the southern shores of Lake Minnetonka.

"Thank God you weren't hurt," Charlie snapped as we exited the highway and he wound our way through the complicated streets surrounding the lake. "I'm starting to think this job of yours might be more trouble than it's worth."

"Hurt? With Sam there?" I laughed. "A person would have to be pretty stupid to take on Sam Barlow in a fight."

Charlie shot me a curious look. "Really? What makes you say that?"

I thought of the hard body I'd felt the night before, the big arms that held me, and Sam's broad, strong chest pressed against mine. "Oh, I don't know," I said vaguely. I looked at the neighborhood we just entered. "I haven't been back here for a long time. Whenever I visited Grandy, I went right to the house and didn't go through town."

"It's changed a lot since we were kids," Charlie said as we drove through the four-block long downtown. "The old houses on the lake are being torn down and mega-mansions are going up."

"They were mansions when we were growing up. How much bigger can a house be?"

"You should see some of them. John's firm bid on a couple of locations and he was telling me about it. They're huge." Charlie turned into the parking lot of the Tedesco Funeral Home, rolling down his window as a man approached the car. "Charles Whittington

112

the Third and Cassandra Whittington," he told the man.

The man gestured us to a side lot where Charlie parked the car and a member of the funeral house staff handed me a placard to put on the dash. I tossed it onto the elm wood interior and got out of the sedan just as Charlie's younger sister, Olivia, pulled into the slot next to us, her sporty red Porsche making Charlie's sleek Jag look like a dowdy old Mom-mobile.

I've always liked Livvie. She's eight years younger than me and as kids growing up we were friends, probably because my mother wouldn't tolerate uppity snobbishness and because C.R. Whittington, Charlie's dad, gave my mother free rein to raise the kids. I give Mom credit for how well the Whittington kids turned out. Without her calm and common-sensed touch, those kids would have been spoiled little monsters. As it was, I married one of them and remained on good terms with all the others except for John, who was born an asshole and stayed one all his life. Three out of four ain't bad, I guess.

"It's good to see you, Cassie." Olivia leaned down and gave me an air kiss, her breath faintly whispering of vermouth. She was a social drunk and probably already had at least one martini to fuel her courage for this ordeal. Straightening, she eyed me critically. "I still can't believe you whacked off all your hair."

I touched my shaggy hair, which had been long and white most of my life and was now short and turning gray. "I couldn't stand it anymore so whacking seemed the thing to do. You're looking good, Livvie." In fact she looked like shit, but I wasn't about to tell her she needed to go up a size in her clothing choices or her hair color was a bit too ashy blonde. Olivia was a law unto herself and always marched to a drummer no one even suspected existed, much less heard. I loved her for it but she was exasperating at times. "I'm glad Grandy Theo went fast without having to suffer through a long illness. It's exactly what she wanted."

Livvie nodded and hugged Charlie when he joined us on my side of the car. "We should all be so lucky," Charlie said, tucking my arm under his. He held out his left arm for Livvie. "Do you want to go in with us?"

Livvie had been a widow for almost eight years and usually went to all family functions alone. "Sure. As long as I don't have to sit next to Diane, I'll let you lead me anywhere."

"I'm not sitting next to her," Charlie warned as we all walked toward the small white building where generations of Whittingtons had been given their final send-off.

I thought of my grim ex-sister-in-law and smiled. "I'll sit next to her," I volunteered. "She hates me so much she'll ignore me."

"True enough." Livvie smiled at the man who held the door for us and led the way into the foyer of the funeral home. "I suppose that's one benefit of being on the family Shit List. You get to avoid all the nasty family members."

"Since I'm not really in the family anymore, it's easy for me," I pointed out. We entered an opulent foyer where people were standing, waiting to be seated.

"You'll always be family, Cassie," Livvie said. "You're more of a sister to me than Rebecca ever was."

"Becky has...issues," I said as the director came out and fussed over us, taking Livvie's fur coat and my more serviceable cloth one.

"Becky's a bitch," Livvie said succinctly. "She needs to let bygones be bygones."

"You did steal her husband." Another man came forward and led us into a large room where a few dozen people already sat, a low buzz of conversation in the air.

"I was just one of many," Livvie said over her shoulder. "Not the first and not the last."

"You were the one he advertised," Charlie said. "At Thanksgiving. Over the pumpkin pie. That's tough to get past, Livvie."

She gave an indolent shrug of one blue-wooled shoulder while we paced down the center aisle. Voices stilled then another murmur of gossip began to stir as we were led to the seats at front and center. I suppose people were surprised to see me there. After all, it was years since I appeared in public with Charlie.

Betty Burke, Grandy's live-in maid and companion, sat in the second row with a young black man whom I recognized as her grandson, a senior in college in Chicago. She probably called him in for moral support when Grandy died. She turned around when she heard the murmur, her dark face creasing into a wide smile when she saw us. Then she turned back to face front, dabbing at her face with a hankie.

As we neared the front of the room the man sitting in the very front row looked back. Charles Richard Whittington the Second eyed me coolly then nodded once. I dipped my head in answer. He gestured to Charlie, who went forward to talk to him as Livvie and I took our seats. I glanced behind me as we sat down and saw the speculative looks on many faces.

I looked at the woman sitting with Charlie's father, directly in front of me. She appeared youngish, probably in her forties. This was the fourth wife, yet another stepmother for Charlie and the kids. "What's her name?" I whispered to Livvie as I settled back in my chair.

"Claire," she whispered back.

Through adroit maneuvering I ended up on the inside of the row, seated next to Diane Whittington, Charlie's acerbic sister-in-law. I settled down, sticking my faux Coach handbag underneath my seat. When I straightened I caught a look of such malevolent distaste on Diane's patrician features I instinctively leaned away. Then she smiled coldly. "What a pleasant surprise. I didn't think we'd see you, Cassie."

I smoothed down the crease in my pants then crossed my legs, my blue Payless loafers a contrast to her elegant high-heeled pumps. "I liked Grandy Theo," I said honestly. "When Charlie asked me to come, I was glad to pay my respects."

"Charles asked you?" Her ice-blue gaze flicked past me to Charlie, who took a seat on the other side of Livvie. "Really?"

"She's in the will," Livvie said loudly. "It makes sense Cassie would attend. We do still plan to have the reading of the will after the service, don't we?"

The silence in the room was so complete I heard someone's wristwatch alarm chime, quickly hushed when it was discovered. In front of us, C.R. the Second stiffened, his broad shoulders like inflexible blocks of stone in his dark gray coat. He was probably seventy years old but he carried his age well, with a haughty elegance combined with his husky, masculine aura. The Second had been a construction foreman when he married Charlie's mother, who was a socialite and heiress. Through clever management he turned her minor fortune into a major one and remade himself at the same time. I respected him but he was still an arrogant son of a bitch.

Diane's husband John leaned over, staring past her at me. He was five years younger than Charlie's fifty-two and was like a distorted image of Charlie: *almost* handsome, *almost* pleasant, *almost* the Golden Boy. His *almost* status had stuck in his craw all his life.

"Glad you could attend, Cassie. How's your gardening job going?"

He made it sound like I was a migrant day laborer. "Fine, John. How are things in the construction business?"

A small gasp of breath told me others around us had heard this exchange. John's company was one of the premier design firms for high-end homes in the Twin Cities. "Fine," he snapped, leaning back.

"Two points to you," Livvie murmured.

"Cassie won the game, set, and match long ago," Charlie grumbled. "Gardening job, my ass. It's like the time he asked you if your software company designed anything except computer graphics used in game programs."

Livvie leaned back and crossed one nylon-clad leg over the other. I envied her long legs and elegant, *Vogue* magazine style. I always felt like a pansy next to a rose whenever I was with a Whittington woman. "Your answer was priceless, too," she said in a low voice. "When you explained your company designed software used by OSHA, I thought he'd have heart failure." She nudged me companionably in the arm. "I still say you should have had someone put in a piece of code that made every house John designed fail inspection."

"I considered it," I admitted. I watched with interest as Rebecca, John's twin sister, entered the funeral home, escorted by her fourth husband. Like all her previous spouses, he was at least fifteen years older than her, distinguished looking, and probably filthy rich. Some women married well. Becky divorced well. I smiled at her and she nodded, a brief smile flickering when she saw me. They sat on the other side of John and Diane, assorted children and grandchildren in the rows behind us all.

"I'm safe," Livvie murmured. "There are three bodies between us."

"Hey, don't count me. I'll duck if it comes to blows."

Livvie sighed loudly. "Matthew wasn't worth such acrimony. He was lousy in bed and even worse at tennis." She said this as though it was a cardinal sin. Of course, for her it was. Livvie was the state women's single tennis champion several years in a row, both as a teenager and as a grown woman. She still played in tennis leagues around the Twin Cities and trounced anyone who came within reach of her bullet-like serve. She and I played doubles once and she effortlessly carried the match, much to my relief. Tennis was not my game despite years of lessons.

Conversation hushed as the minister came out to speak. I was glad Grandy Theo wasn't being buried from a church. She was a staunch agnostic all her life and I'm sure she insisted on this kind of service—brief, to the point, and only a tiny bit teary.

Mid-way through the ceremony, C.R. turned and looked at us, nodding toward the front. We kids all stood and trooped to stand before the crowd. We lined up, then the four siblings all turned to me, waiting for my cue.

I took a deep breath and launched into *Amazing Grace* a cappella and for a few moments we all set aside our gripes and fell into our childhood roles as we sang the song that was always sung at just about every 'going-away' in the family. Charlie's tenor joined my soprano after a few bars then John's baritone voice joined in, supported by the two girls who sang alto softly in the background. We had sung this song countless times growing up and it was natural for me to slip my arms through John's and

Charlie's while the girls stood next to them. We finished with all the voices fading away and with me singing the first verse again, solo.

Then the siblings stepped back and I launched into the songs Granny Theo had requested, first the Judy Collins one then the Billie Holiday classic *I'll Be Seeing You*. Charlie sang with me the way we did so many times before. I remembered the first time I heard that song, playing on the old phonograph in Grandy's Shorewood mansion. I borrowed it to listen at home and the next time I came for Saturday tea, I sang the song to Grandy Theo. That was when the grown-ups discovered I had an excellent singing voice and I started taking lessons.

The siblings joined in with me on the final verse then we fell silent. I had poignant childhood memories of times like this when we children sang together as a group. I saw the hazy mist of memory in the eyes of the others as we finished and went back to our seats.

Next C.R. gravely accepted the urn of ashes from the minister. Probably only the family knew he wanted to dump them on the nearest garbage heap. Grandy Theo hated C.R. with a passion and tried to discourage Gloria, her only daughter, from marrying him. Theo later forgave Gloria when she produced grandchildren, but her animosity to C.R. never abated.

"What's next?" I asked Livvie.

"Now we go to the house and have drinks then read the will." She picked up her chic little leather handbag, an exact match for her blue jacket and skirt. "Grandy wanted us to fling her from the boat this summer, so we're planning a party to do it. I'll make sure you're invited."

We fell into step behind C.R., who led the way up the aisle with his family arrayed behind him like a bridal train. There was an awkward moment at the front of the church when Rebecca came face to face with Livvie, but I quickly interposed myself between the two and averted a possible brawl.

As we stood on the front step and waited for the cars to be brought to us, John came up behind me. "I heard you're involved in a murder investigation, Cassie." His voice carried loudly over the people who were leaving the service, their voices lowered and hushed.

I looked back at him. He stood on the step above me, smiling politely. I saw the cold dislike in his pale hazel eyes. "Not really."

"Really? That's not what I heard." He paused then said, "Of course, given your family history, I wouldn't be surprised."

Well, so much for lovely childhood memories. I took a swing at him and all hell broke loose.

Chapter 11

"I'm appalled at your behavior today," C.R. Whittington the Second intoned as we sat in the library at the family home on Lake Minnetonka. "Your grandmother would be appalled, too."

"Bullshit," Livvie slurred. She was on her second martini. Or perhaps I should say she was on the second martini that I knew of. There may have been others prior to the ones I saw her consume. "Grandy Theo would have applauded. John was completely out of line."

"So was Cassie," Diane spat. "She took a swing at John."

"And missed," Rebecca pointed out.

"Not for want of trying," John said, his voice supercilious and cold. "Of course, violence runs in her family."

I started to rise from the chair where Charlie pushed me just a few minutes earlier. Before I could get far, though, he put a hand on my shoulder. "One more crack like that, John and I'll hit you myself." His hand tightened. "Apologize. Right now."

"I will not. Her father was responsible for—"

"I will not have this discussed." The Second's

voice cut through the squabbling like a dose of cold water. "Cassie's mother was a kind and loving person who raised you all to act better than this. Honor her memory by doing as she taught." He sat behind his big oak desk, holding court like the despot he was, his dark green eyes looking first at me then at John, who stood near the fireplace.

His tone of voice brooked no argument. John shot me a hate-filled stare. I returned it in full measure. Then I settled back, Charlie's hand still on my shoulder. I touched it, reassured by his contact. "It's okay, C.R.," I murmured. "I won't hurt him."

He leaned over and kissed me on the cheek. "I wouldn't let you dirty your hands," he whispered in my ear.

"You get 'em, Uncle Charlie," Becky's teenaged son Cory whispered from his spot on the couch nearby. His younger brother nudged him and Cory winked at me before turning his attention back to the Nintendo game in his hands. The older grandkids ignored us. They were familiar with our family disputes.

"Now if we could continue with this afternoon's business," C.R. said, looking to his right. On cue a young woman stood and walked forward. She was dressed in what I thought of as 'lawyer clothes': a dark skirt, white blouse, and dark jacket, all of which were professional but also feminine. She was tall and slender, probably in her thirties or early forties, with black hair pulled back into a severe bun and blue eyes hidden by dark-rimmed glasses which caught and reflected back the light in the room. C.R. nodded to her. "This is Janelle Rimes. She was Theo's lawyer and she's here to read Theo's last will and testament."

I put on an attentive face although I was seething inside. John's crack about my parentage hurt, probably because I just talked about it last night with Sam. It was years since the past had been raked up and brought to light.

"...beloved friend, Betty Burke, the photo album so designated with her name. In addition, I bequeath Betty a trust fund of one hundred thousand dollars, to be used as she deems necessary. I have also made provisions for her living arrangements, to be discussed later in this document."

I looked up, belatedly realizing some words were being spoken. The lawyer droned through a series of bequests to friends then she came to the family, her eyes darting from Livvie to John to Becky. When her gaze came to Charlie, it lingered slightly and I hid a smile. Many women had that reaction to Charlie.

"To my granddaughter, Olivia Whittington Carlyle, I leave my collections of china and crystal so she might have a suitable means to entertain her friends."

Livvie smiled and raised her martini glass. "Thank you, Grandy. I appreciate it." I think she was even sincere.

"To my granddaughter, Rebecca Whittington Stark, I leave my diaries and scrapbooks which chronicle several of the disappointments I've endured in my life. I hope she will learn from them."

Becky appeared faintly amused but her husband looked put out, as though he'd expected something more substantial from the old lady. I suppose whenever a rich person died, the vultures all started circling.

"...grandson, John, I leave my shares in his design company, which I purchased years ago to assist him in getting his start in business."

I hid a smile. The shares were next to useless because John owned the majority of the stock in the company. I suppose it was nice he would have 99.9% of the stock, though. A look at his face told me he, like Becky's husband, expected far more from this day and from the old lady who died.

The lawyer cleared her throat. "To my beloved grandson, Charles, I leave two of my prized collections: the one of Hummel figurines and the other, my collection of software stock." She raised her eyes from the paper and looked at Charlie, two bright spots of pink color standing out on her pale cheeks.

There was a silence in the room then the import of the words soaked in. "Stock?" John demanded.

The lawyer looked at him, her eyes cool and distant behind her businesslike dark-rimmed glasses. "Mrs. Penningford had an impressive portfolio." Then she smiled at Charlie, giving him a look of conspiratorial mischief that made me grin. The look vanished almost instantly behind a brisk façade.

Charlie squeezed my shoulder. "I always told her the future was in technology. I guess she listened to me."

The lawyer looked at his hand on my shoulder and her face seemed to flatten, her faintly Asian features stiffening. She nodded briskly, her eyes going back to the papers she held. "Your grandmother had a nice portfolio with Microsoft, Intel, Oracle, and Nintendo, some of which have had stock splits over the years."

John looked like he was struggling not to scream. I peered up at Charlie. "Nice to know she took your advice."

"And to my granddaughter-by-proxy, Cassandra Roberta Wheelock Whittington, I leave the balance of my estate, including my homes in Shorewood, Minnesota and Naples, Florida as well as the cabin on Lake Vermillion in Northern Minnesota. Cassie's friendship has been a constant joy in my life for almost fifty years, since she came to live with us as a small child. I always enjoyed our Saturday afternoon tea, which she never missed regardless of how busy she was. I've valued her love and her friendship deeply. As a provision of this bequest, I ask that Cassie allow Betty Burke to remain in the home in Shorewood as long as Betty so desires and if Betty chooses to leave, that Cassie sees to it Betty is provided with a proper home and retirement income."

I turned my head slowly to stare at the lawyer, my jaw sagging open. "What?"

"What?" John's shout was certainly louder than my whisper.

Livvie started to laugh, the giggle soon turning into a guffaw. After a second Becky joined in. Charlie was grinning and I knew he wished he could join his sisters.

I looked around the room, my eyes huge. Betty smiled and the Second looked bemused. "That's not right," I said weakly. "There must be a lot of money there. I mean, it's not right. I'm not her family or—"

"The estate was probated at approximately fifteen million dollars." The lawyer smiled briefly at me then looked at Charlie. Some message passed between them then she looked at me again. "Of course, we'll need to deduct the items she left to other family members. And the real estate isn't included in the estimation because of market fluctuations and..."

I didn't hear the rest. Grandy Theo left me fifteen million dollars? My ears were buzzing and I was dizzy, the room spinning around me.

Charlie leaned over. "I think you can afford to buy that Jaguar now."

****

"You knew about this, didn't you?" I demanded as Charlie drove me home.

Charlie nodded. "Grandy told me about it ten years ago when she set it up."

"It's not right," I said for the umpteenth time. "I'm not family and it's a lot of money."

"You know as well as I do that none of us need the money, no matter what John says or Becky's husband says. Gran wanted to do this." He looked at Barlow's Nursery, coming up in the distance on the right. "What will you do with the money?"

"I guess I'll figure it out on Monday." On his advice and the advice of his father, I was meeting with lawyers from Charlie's law firm on Monday afternoon to go over the details. I also had an appointment with Charlie's financial advisor for later in the week to help me figure out what to do. "I can't comprehend it. Fifteen million?" I stared at the main building where Sam Barlow and I were trapped the night before, my thoughts bouncing around like a pinball.

"You don't have to work now, you know."

"Of course I do. I mean, I told them I'd work for them so..." I shook my head. "I'm not sure what I mean. I guess I don't believe it." He turned the corner and I looked anxiously at the nursery parking lot, but didn't see Sam's car. I remembered his words from the night before. "Both Kathleen and Sam think we haven't gotten over our marriage," I said, the words slipping out before I could restrain them.

"Both Kathleen and Sam are wrong." I knew Charlie well enough to hear the underlying anger in his flippant voice.

"Do you think we're letting the past have too much effect on our present?"

Charlie turned into the townhouse development where I lived. "Our past has affected everyone in our family, Cassie. It's inevitable. I think we've all done a damn good job of putting it behind us."

"Except John," I muttered.

"John's a jerk and always has been. He was pissed off when you and I got married because he

126

had a crush on you."

"John?" I demanded incredulously. "Impossible. I was always the nanny's kid to him, just scum of the earth."

"Wrong, oh Clueless Wonder." Charlie grinned at me as he pulled the Jag into my driveway. "He had the hots for you. He got over it, of course, but I think he's still hostile because you married me."

I shook my head, bemused by this day and all the happenings. "Sam asked me out for coffee tomorrow. I'm not sure if I should go or not. He's the owner. It might look bad."

"You can buy and sell his place a hundred times over. Don't worry about it."

I considered it as I got out of the car and walked to the door, Charlie by my side. "I just don't want to be accused of any workplace misconduct."

"What are you worried about? If you care what the other staffers think, ask them how they feel. I think I can guarantee you they won't mind." Charlie pulled me to him, hugging me tightly. "You're a smart, funny, sexy woman, C.R.W. You need to realize that." He leaned back slightly and looked down at me. "And you're a rich woman now. You'll have to be careful. You'll have gold diggers coming out of the woodwork."

I hugged him, pushing my face against his jacket front and inhaling the comforting scent of his aftershave. "I never wanted to be rich, Charlie. I'll miss her. She's all we have left of our past, all that's left of our childhood."

"There's my father," he murmured, his breath warm on my forehead.

"Your father is doing everything he can to forget the past," I grumbled. "It's not the same and you know it."

Charlie kissed me lightly. "I knew what you meant. We'll always be family, Cassie, you and me."

He gave me a little shove toward my door. "Let me know if you have any questions about being a millionaire."

I laughed. "Thanks, Charlie. I probably will have."

"And Cassie?"

I turned to look back at him. He was regarding me with an odd look, sort of hopeful combined with worry. "What, Charlie?"

"Are you going to go out with Sam Barlow?"

"For coffee, yes. Anything else?" I shrugged. "I'm not sure. I'll see where my hormones take me."

Charlie smiled but it looked forced. "Get those condoms ready, then."

I grinned, too, and went into the house, my brain stuffed full of ideas and shock. Fifteen million dollars? The figure was impossible to understand. I went into the bedroom and shed my funeral duds, pulling on old ripped blue jeans and my *What part of' I Don't Give a Crap' don't you understand?* sweatshirt. I looked around the modest townhouse as I wandered into the kitchen where Houdini basked in late afternoon sun.

"I don't have to work anymore," I told him as I poured myself a glass of wine from the Wine in a Box on the counter. He yawned and stretched, making himself look like a horizontal SuperCat taking off in a single bound. "I can sleep in like you and take vacations. I don't have to worry about money." He yawned again, obviously unworried as long as the kibble kept flowing and the sun kept shining.

I plopped down in my faux oak kitchen chair and looked around the room. Everything here was purchased either second-hand or from big box stores like Kmart or Target, with an occasional splurge at a discount furniture mart. I could buy real antiques now if I wanted. I could drink wine from a bottle with a cork and buy shoes at Nordstrom's. I saw my car keys lying on the counter. Despite Charlie's teasing, I wouldn't buy a Jag, but...

I took my wine and went into the den, Houdini padding after me. I loaded up my CD player and clicked on Crosby, Stills, and Nash, humming along with "Helplessly Hoping" as I fired up my computer. Charlie and I sang that song to each other at our wedding and it still occupied a special place in my heart.

I took a long sip of wine and watched my computer come to life. I've always had a secret hankering for a Mini-Cooper and I decided to indulge some wishful thinking. I happily clicked my way to the Mini web site where I spent an amusing half-hour designing a new car for myself as I sang along with CSN, then Carly Simon, then Eric Clapton. Even after pimping a car outrageously, I still hadn't 'spent' a ton of money—at least, a ton compared to fifteen million dollars, but certainly more than what I was accustomed to spending in one fell swoop.

I leaned back and propped my feet up on the desk, which wobbled alarmingly. I pulled over a notepad and started making a list. "New desk," I told Houdi, who settled onto the corner near my printer and peered intently out the window. "New chair, new computer." I grinned. "New TV and stereo, too. A Blackberry. Or maybe an iPhone. Yeah."

The Blackberry made me think of Charlie and of Sam, each of whom owned such a gadget. I once attended a writing seminar when I had the misguided notion I could write a romance novel. The speaker, a New York Times bestselling author, talked about alpha and beta males. I had no idea such designations existed, but seeing Sam and Charlie together made the whole thing clear. Sam was definitely alpha and Charlie was definitely beta. Both were sexy, charming, and different as night from day. Charlie was summer—all warm, fun and easy to love. Sam was winter, tough to love but invigorating and exciting.

"What did you think of Sam Barlow?" I asked Houdi.

His ears flickered but he remained staring outside. The motion made me remember another option for my newfound wealth. I started a new page on my pad and made a note of charities I could now donate to, the local Animal Shelter at the top of the list. "I could give money to the school for scholarships," I muttered as I stood to get a refill on my wine. "I could donate to a woman's shelter and the school and the horticulture society."

Houdi didn't look away from whatever caught his attention. I paused as I left the room, almost stumbling over a pile of printer paper on the floor. It had grown dark while I sat there, ogling sports cars and indulging in monetary fantasies. I looked over his head, peering at the front yard.

A pickup truck was at the curb.

I jerked back so fast I almost overbalanced. As it was, I had to do an intricate dance on the slippery pile of paper in order to keep from slamming into the window. When I finally recovered my equilibrium, I peeked over Houdi's head, wishing belatedly I had taken the time to install the curtains on the window. It was such a quiet street, though, and I had no neighbors directly across from me and I was studying for finals and one thing or another always came up. Of course, excuses were hollow now that I needed something to lurk behind and had nothing.

The streetlight cast a circular yellow glow down to the curb, but the front of the truck was just out of its circumference. There was a faint mist in the air, too, the product of today's quota of melting snow and the cooling night temperatures. I thought I saw someone in the front seat, but wasn't sure. I had only glimpsed the truck the other day, but this one looked bigger, more ominous somehow. I tilted my head, trying for a different angle. Was this one a lighter color? Why would someone be sitting outside my house? Of course, why had some man tried to molest a woman when she returned home from the park the other day? I was as good a target as anybody.

What to do? I didn't have a phone in this room. The nearest one was in the kitchen. I scurried through the foyer and back into the kitchen. I ducked below counter level and bobbed my way to the phone on the far wall, near the fridge. I snagged the receiver, almost upending the charging base in my haste. I dialed 911 as headlights suddenly glowed in front of my house, shining into the room.

Was the Pervert moving in for the kill? As I waited for the dispatcher to pick up, I strained to hear anything. All I heard was an ominous silence outside.

"911, what's your emergency?" I didn't recognize this voice. It was a man, sounding bored and a bit stuffed up, like he had a head cold.

"I think the Pickaway Pervert is outside my house," I said breathlessly as I inched my way toward the front door.

"Where are you, ma'am?" Even with this startling pronouncement from me he still sounded bored. Maybe they'd been getting Pervert calls often.

I gave my address and added, "There's someone in my driveway. And I saw a car at the curb, just sitting there."

"We'll have a police officer drive by your house."

I clicked the phone off and tiptoed to the front door, peeking through the spyhole. The motion light had come on outside and I saw a sporty red Benz parked in my driveway.

I backed away from the door, almost falling over

Houdini, who stared raptly at the door. I didn't know anybody who owned a red Benz. I peeked out again as the cell phone in my pocket thumped. I pulled it out and opened it. "Hello?" I whispered.

"Cassie, it's Sam. How did it go today at the funeral?"

"There's somebody outside my house. It's like the other day. There's a truck sitting there. And somebody just pulled into my driveway."

"Did you call the police?"

"Yeah, I just did. They said—" I heard a car door slam and footsteps on the walk outside. "Somebody's coming," I whispered, ducking low.

"I'm coming over. I'll be there in a few minutes."

I closed the phone, not bothering to acknowledge his help. I took one more step back as the doorbell pealed, the bells right above my head in the foyer. I almost peed my pants. Would the Pervert ring a doorbell? The bell rang again. Houdi planted himself in front of me, staring up at the doorknob as though daring it to turn.

And damned if it didn't turn. I dropped the portable phone and lunged for the knob, belatedly realizing I didn't lock it behind me when I came home in the afternoon, my head stuffed full of thoughts of money and men. As I grabbed the door, Houdi made a break for it. "Get back here," I hissed, lunging for his disappearing hindquarters.

A woman pushed the door open, tangled with my cat, and started falling toward me. I caught a quick glimpse of her face. She was vaguely familiar but I didn't have time to decipher what I was seeing. I dropped below her reach, tackled Houdini, and fell across my front step with a wiggling cat in my arms and Kathleen Emerson, Charlie's ex-girlfriend, landing on top of me.

The pickup truck parked on the street was making a U-turn in my cul-de-sac. As I clamped my arms around my cat, I had a birds-eye view of a squad car barreling toward the truck, lights flashing and sirens blaring.

Then my head hit the pavement, I saw stars, and the world went black.

Chapter 12

I was unconscious so briefly it was like a long eye-blink. When I was cognizant again, I had a clawing cat clasped to my bosom, a woman lying on top of me, and a police officer running up my front walk.

"Get off me!" I struggled to push Kathleen away from my legs as I clamped down hard on Houdi's back end and wrapped my arms around him.

"You didn't need to call the police," she yelled as she kicked at me.

"Ouch! Stop it! Let me up!" I scrambled to my feet, tearing the knees of my old blue jeans even further. I pushed into the house just as the patrolman reached me.

"Are you okay, ma'am?" he demanded, grabbing Kathleen's arm and hauling her to her feet.

"It's my house." I turned to the right and tossed Houdi into the den, slamming the door behind him. "She's the intruder."

"I did not intrude!"

"Bullshit! You pushed your way into my house." I looked out at the street where a squad car was parked at the curb. The pickup truck was nowhere in sight. "Did you get him? Where'd he go?" Another squad car pulled into my drive beside the red Benz and a pink-faced young officer got out, hurrying to the townhouse next door. "Where's he going?"

"Let's go inside, ma'am," the patrol officer said, gesturing toward my foyer. He was a solid-looking, bulky man with brown hair and alert blue eyes. "I called in another officer. He's talking to the owner of the truck."

I took a couple of steps out onto the sidewalk and peered to my left. The suspicious pickup truck was parked three houses down in a driveway. In the light from the open garage door I could see the other officer approaching, obviously talking to the man in the truck although I couldn't hear the words being exchanged. "Damn, is that a neighbor?"

"Don't you know who lives next to you?" Kathleen demanded, throwing back her shoulders and thrusting her large chest, well-clothed in a leather jacket, at the officer.

"I just moved here." I pushed past her and went toward the rattling den door, where I heard the sound of a cat clawing. "I haven't met everybody yet. What the hell are you doing here?"

"Do you know each other?" the officer asked, glancing at his partner, who was just coming up my walk.

"She's dating my ex-husband." I leaned over to examine the tear in my jeans.

"Domestic dispute," the cop said to the younger officer who was approaching.

"Like hell it's a domestic dispute," I objected. "She pushed her way into my house."

"The door wasn't locked." Kathleen crossed her arms under her bosom, giving her equipment a subtle lift. The two men glanced at the objects in question then back to me, their faces blandly curious.

"An oversight on my part." I considered countering with my own womanly charms but they were hidden under an oversized sweatshirt. "Who's the guy in the truck? I guess it wasn't the Pervert, huh?"

"He lives down the street. He had his truck parked outside while he did some work in the garage," the younger officer said. "Besides, we caught the Pervert. It'll be in Monday's paper."

"Really?" After psyching myself up for an attack, I was starting to feel a bit deflated. "Well, good. Sorry about the false alarm."

"No problem. Better to be safe than sorry." The older officer looked pointedly at Kathleen. "Is everything okay now?"

I looked at my rattling den door, visions of clawed furniture and chewed printer cords dancing in my brain. "We're fine. I'll handle this."

Kathleen glared at me. "I came over to talk about our problem."

"We don't have a problem, Kathleen. You do." I escorted the two officers out to the stoop. "My ex broke up with her and she blames me." I shrugged. "Go figure."

They were well-trained men, keeping their faces impassive as they probably mentally contrasted short, poorly dressed and older me to mid-thirties, buxom, blonde, stylish Kathleen. "If there's a problem, we'd be glad to stay," the younger one offered.

We all three turned as Sam's maroon SUV pulled up in my driveway behind the red Benz. "I've got back-up," I said as Sam got out and hurried toward us.

He put an arm around my shoulders and I leaned into his comforting embrace. "I got here as fast as I could," he said.

It seemed the most natural thing in the world to

look up at him and meet his lips in a quick kiss. "Thanks, Sam. It's okay, though. Turns out it was a false alarm."

He looked past me to the front door where Kathleen was framed, shooting malevolent eye-daggers at us. "Problems?"

"Charlie's ex-girlfriend." I stuck out a hand to the police officers. "Thanks for coming, I appreciate it."

They each handed me a business card then got into their squad cars, pulling away as Sam and I turned to go into the house. We hadn't gone two steps, though, when Charlie's Jag pulled onto the street, executing a neat U-turn and parking at the curb. "Oh, for cryin'—" I hurried across the damp lawn to meet him. "Charlie, what are you doing here?"

"Kathleen told me to meet you here." He slammed the Jag door hard. Like me, he had changed clothes and was now wearing jeans and a gray sweater. Unlike me, though, his jeans were crisply ironed and his sweater fit him like a glove. He looked down at my knees. "What happened?"

I followed his gaze and saw an ooze of blood. "Kathleen and I tangled on the steps."

"Damn it, I'm going to—" He strode past me and Sam into my house.

Sam put an arm around me again. "Ready to face the past?"

I shook my head. "This is impossible."

He grinned suddenly, looking like an impish little boy who was getting ready to watch the grown-ups act like idiots. "Trust me. It's very possible."

I walked into the house, Sam by my side. Charlie and Kathleen were standing in the foyer about a foot apart, glaring at each other.

"Do you guys want some privacy?" I asked. "You can go into the kitchen."

"No way," Kathleen interrupted. "This involves you, too, Cassie." Her gaze shifted to Sam and her features softened. The flirtatious woman was back, replacing the shrill, angry bitch who was there just a second before. "Who are you?"

"Sam Barlow." He extended a hand. "An interested bystander."

I shot him a warning look. He gave me a wide-eyed, innocent smile as he shook Kathleen's hand. She smiled in return, her blue eyes assessing him quickly from head to toe. I think she liked what she saw because she moved a bit closer to him.

"This is totally out of line," Charlie snapped. "You have no right to involve Cassie in our problems."

"Cassie is the problem," Kathleen said, obviously remembering her role as wronged girlfriend. She strode into the living room, tracking mud onto my hardwood floors.

"Come in," I muttered. "Make yourself at home." I looked at Charlie and shrugged. "Anybody want a beer? A glass of wine?" I opened the den door and Houdi shot out, took one look at the now-closed front door, and came to a screeching halt. He looked over his shoulder, turned, and meandered into the living room to check out the female stranger on his turf, the epitome of feline sangfroid.

"Kathleen is allergic to cats," Charlie said in a low voice.

"What a pity." I grabbed my empty wine glass from the den and went into the kitchen, Sam trailing behind me.

"I'll take a beer." He went to the fridge and pulled it open.

"Help yourself." I watched as he peered inside. He was wearing black jeans and a black and white flannel shirt and I had to admit, he looked as good as Charlie did, but in a different, more outdoorsy, way.

I could see why Kathleen gave him the old one-two.

Charlie came in. "I'm sorry, Cassie. She just won't understand."

"I guess I won't understand either," Sam said as he straightened up, holding a bottle of Old Peculier. "Interesting beer," he commented to me.

I opened the E.T.C. drawer and rooted around inside, finally emerging with my Mickey Mouse bottle opener, which I handed to him. "It suits my mood now and again," I said.

"What do you mean, you don't understand either?" Charlie demanded.

"I said I *won't* understand but maybe I should rephrase it." Sam went unerringly to my glasses cupboard and pulled down one of my big tumblers. Charlie watched this action with narrowed eyes, probably wondering, as was I, how Sam was making himself right at home. Then I remembered Sam watching me as I put things away in the kitchen the other night. He must have mentally cataloged my cupboards then.

Sam poured his beer and took a sip. "I can't understand how two such intelligent people can ignore what's right in front of them."

"I'm sure you'll explain," Charlie said acidly, crossing his arms on his chest and leaning back in the doorway, his green eyes flicking from Sam to me.

I struggled to keep my face as bland as possible. Charlie seldom got mad, but when he did, it was memorable. I recognized the signs. He was working himself into a snit. The best thing I could do was keep quiet and try to get rid of Sam and Kathleen as soon as possible.

"You love Cassie. She loves you. I think a lot of what she feels is tangled up with what happened to both of you years ago, but part of it is about her youth, too. You guys got married when you were in college, and—"

"That's crap." Charlie straightened, keeping his arms still rigidly crossed. I suspect it was because he wanted to shake Sam, who by contrast looked totally relaxed, leaning back against my stove and sipping his beer as though it was a typical Saturday night. "You don't know anything about Cassie and me."

Sam looked at me, his dark eyes searching my face. I met his gaze squarely. "I've gotten to know Cassie in the last day or two," he said softly. "I'd like to get to know her even better."

"Charlie? Charlie, there's a cat in here!" Kathleen's voice had an edge of panic to it and I wondered fleetingly if she was one of those women who feared animals no matter how benign the animal appeared.

"The rocket scientist speaks." I refilled my wine glass at the box spigot, my hand trembling slightly. "You'd better get in there and rescue her from Houdini, the killer monster cat."

"Kathleen can fend for herself," Charlie snapped. I flinched at his tone, slopping wine over the rim of my glass. He winced but didn't apologize. Charlie was building up a full head of steam and nothing was going to stop him. "Cassie will always be a big part of my life because of our childhood and what we went through together. We may have gotten married for all the wrong reasons, but it doesn't mean we have to hate each other." His gaze moved to me. "I want her to be happy. Now that she has her inheritance, I know she'll have the freedom to make choices she couldn't make before. Now she doesn't have to worry about money and what effect it might have on her choices."

I tensed. "I don't know what you mean, Charlie."

"Charlie! I can't get away from this cat!"

Sam grinned. "Typical cat. He's gone right to the person who hates him." He sipped his beer. "What inheritance, Cassie?"

I ignored him and focused on Charlie, who watched me the way Houdini watched the birds out on the deck, his face still but predatory. "You don't have to work now, Cassie," he said. "You can travel. You have freedom to do what you want." He hesitated then said, "Money doesn't have to be an issue with you anymore."

I frowned, not sure what he was saying. It was true, I always felt awkward around him and the other Whittingtons because of their money and my lack thereof, but I don't think it ever interfered with my feelings for them. I shoved the thought aside for later examination. I had other problems to deal with now.

"I always had freedom, Charlie. It may not seem that way to you, but I did. I'm working at what I want to do." I glanced at Sam, who looked at me with his dark, unfathomable eyes. "If I don't like it, I can leave."

Houdini sauntered into the room, pausing long enough to sniff at Sam's boots and rub against Charlie's ankles. Then he came to me and sat down, staring at me with regal intentness. I turned to the kibble cupboard and got out the box but before I could answer His Majesty's summons, my cell phone, stuffed back in my pocket, thumped. I fumbled it out as I followed Houdi to his dishes in the mudroom.

"Gidget, it's Aaron. I wanted to ask you something."

I dumped some food into Houdi's dish and straightened, eyeing Charlie and Sam, talking in low voices in the kitchen just a few feet away. The hum of the nearby refrigerator and the purring of my cat echoed in the small space, making it difficult for me to eavesdrop.

"This isn't a very good time, Aaron. I'm busy." I leaned toward the men in time to hear Sam say, "...but I won't take a chance if she's still tied to you."

141

"Now just a minute," I said, pulling the phone away from my face and striding back to the two combatants. "You can't talk about me as if I'm not here."

"Charlie?" Kathleen peered around the doorway into the kitchen. "Where's da'anima?" she asked, her voice so clogged it was almost impossible to understand her.

"Good of you to join us, Kathleen, since you were the one who started this little party," Charlie said harshly. He gave her a dismissive look, his gaze turning immediately back to Sam and me.

I blinked in surprise at the sight of the previously model-pretty woman. She was weeping, her face puffy and red and her nose running. Small pink dots puckered her cheeks and her forehead looked like an advertisement for acne cream.

Sam plucked a square of paper towel from the holder on the kitchen counter and handed it to her without comment.

"Tank dew," she sobbed, dabbing at her face.

"...what to do," a voice in my ear said. I jerked in surprise. I forgot all about poor Aaron. "I'm afraid she may have done something. I thought I was responsible but..."

"I resent your intrusion like this, Kathleen," Charlie grated. He swung around to glare at Sam, who held his beer glass so tightly I was surprised it didn't break. It was the only sign of tension Sam exhibited. His face remained calm, immobile and curious as Charlie snapped, "And yours, Barlow."

"Doesn't anyone care what I want?" I demanded, leaning on the kitchen island separating me from the men and Kathleen, weeping in the doorway.

They apparently didn't care because everyone continued to ignore me. I heard a noise from the phone in my hand. I put it back to my ear in time to hear Aaron say, "...should I? I'm not sure it's the right thing to do."

"I think you should," I said immediately. "Always go with your first instinct." I pulled the phone away and glared at Kathleen. "I'd appreciate it if you'd leave."

Sam's head swung so he could stare at me. "And me?" I hesitated. He smiled slowly, little lines appearing around his warm, dark eyes. "Cassie?" he asked softly.

I put the phone back to my ear. "...an accident. Do you think they'll believe me?"

"I'm sure they will, Aaron," I said soothingly. "Can we talk more about this later? I'm sort of busy."

"You're right. I'll do it." He sounded relieved, as though I had confirmed some thought of his. I wondered what it was I just agreed to. "Thanks, Gidget." The line went quiet.

"Do what?" I muttered, folding the phone.

Kathleen glared at me as she dabbed at her face, the runny mascara giving her raccoon eyes. "You hab a cat," she sniffed.

"No shit, Sherlock." I looked down at the culprit who was merrily munching at his kibble. "Sorry you're allergic." I tried hard to inject sincerity in my voice but know I failed utterly when I saw her exasperated glare.

"I hab to leab." She wiped at her weeping eyes then turned to Sam, who handed her another square of towel. "Wudju move your cah?"

Sam put his beer down. "I'll be right back," he told me.

I nodded, hazarding a glance at Charlie, who was glaring at him. "Give me a minute," I said to Sam. "Charlie and I need to talk."

Sam nodded and put a hand under Kathleen's arm, steering her out to the foyer. Houdi, alert to the sound of an opening door, started to dart by me but I grabbed him and held on until I heard the front door open and close.

Charlie pushed away from the wall. "I'm sorry, Cassie."

I pushed Houdi into the laundry room and closed the door. "I'm sorry, too, Charlie. You shouldn't have had to come out here again." A yowl of anger and the crash of a ceramic dish told me I'd have some cat food to clean up soon. Then I heard another dish and winced. I amended that thought. I would have water mixed with cat food and would have a soggy mess to clean up.

I ambled toward the kitchen doorway and the front foyer. "I'm sorry about Kathleen, too. I think she really cares about you."

He put an arm around my shoulders. "No matter what she says, I didn't break up with her because of you. I don't want you to feel badly about it." His solid hand on my shoulder was comforting and I appreciated what he said, even though I wasn't sure if I believed it. "Kathleen was too possessive. It wasn't going to work, not matter what." We reached the front door and I heard CS&N singing on my stereo in the den. My CDs had re-cycled and were starting again.

"Our wedding song," Charlie whispered when we heard the three male voices harmonizing. He pulled me to him and looked down at me, his green eyes sad and puzzled. "I love you, Cassie."

I put my arms around him. "I love you, Charlie. I always will." I hugged him hard then looked up at him, startling a look of such longing in his eyes I tried to move back.

Instead of releasing me, he pulled me roughly to him, his arms tight around me. His hand cupped my neck, pulling my head back. Then his lips came down on mine.

I felt his longing, his passion in every tearing instant of his kiss.

144

Then his arms loosened and he almost ran out the door, passing Sam on the sidewalk outside my house.

I clung to the doorway, stunned.

Charlie was still in love with me.

Chapter 13

I didn't have time to consider the implications of Charlie's kiss. Sam came into the foyer and took me in his arms. "I'm not backing down, Cassie," he said, his eyes intent on mine. "I won't give up without a fight."

"Give up what?" I saw Charlie out of the corner of my eye, striding down my sidewalk to his dark Jaguar.

"You."

Sam's tone of voice pulled my eyes back to him. I nudged the door closed with one foot. "I don't know what to feel, Sam," I said honestly. "I've just met you."

He grinned suddenly. "I'll be honest with you," he whispered, his lips tantalizingly close to my ear. "I just want sex now. We can talk about love and all that later, but right now..." He brushed a kiss against my ear lobe and I shivered. "I want you." His hands slipped under my sweatshirt and I gasped as he started to manipulate the hooks of my bra.

His blunt words awakened a fire in me. He was right. I would worry about details later. Right now I had a man in my arms and I was anxious to explore my options. I drew him close to me. "The bedroom is that way." I jerked my head to the right.

Sam stared into my eyes. "Are you doing this just to prove you don't love Charlie?"

"I don't know why I'm doing this," I admitted. "I'm horny and I want you. That's all I know right now."

His dark brown eyes were searching, looking at me so intently I felt already stripped naked. "Oh, hell. It's good enough for me," he growled. He picked me up in his arms. "And there's a perfectly good couch straight ahead."

We were in the living room in a few strides and he set me down before kicking off his boots, which landed with a clatter near the windows. I fumbled with clothing, tugging off my sweatshirt and bra before he even turned back to me. I felt a brief moment of insecurity. I wasn't kidding with Charlie before. I hadn't been with a man since I lost almost seventy pounds, and I wasn't sure what reaction I would get. Plus it was almost a decade since I slept with anyone and a lot can happen to a woman in that time.

Sam's eyes widened when he saw me and he smiled slowly. "Nice to know you're anxious," he murmured, his hands going to the buttons of his shirt.

"Let me." I sat up but he gently pushed me back down, his hand on my shoulder sliding down to cup my left breast.

"I can do it faster." His voice was hoarse and warm. And he was right. In seconds he stripped off the flannel shirt, revealing a tight black T-shirt underneath. My thoughts about his physical fitness were right. His chest looked rock hard and solid.

"Do you work out?" I asked, running my hand up over his abdomen as he snaked the shirt off over his head.

"Every day," he said, his voice muffled. He tossed the T-shirt aside then carefully pulled off his glasses, setting them on the end table near my head. Lying next to me, his hand went to the waistband of my jeans. "Can I?" he asked as he kissed his way slowly down my neck to my breast.

"Please do." The hard little knobs of his nipples sprang to attention under my touch. His body was solid and I felt the ripple of muscle on his arms as I ran my hands over him. I wondered if he could feel my heat and wetness as he pushed my jeans downward and cupped my body in his hand. He made a low noise in this throat when he slipped a finger under my panties and started to probe me.

His hardness pressed on my leg, the long solid length of him in his jeans. I leaned back, opening my legs and reveling in the feelings his fingers were evoking. It had been so long since I felt this sexy, this wanton. I moved my hips under him, my eyes intent on his as he excited me, making my body remember what it felt like as he brought me slowly to the brink of orgasm.

I suddenly remembered.

Condoms.

I saw the knowledge flare in his eyes, too. "Damn," he muttered. "I'm not sure if I have—"

I grinned. "By chance, I'm prepared. Hold on." I wiggled out from under him and started to walk out of the room. I glanced back to see Sam lying on the couch, staring at me with a bemused look on his face. "Why don't you get comfortable while I'm gone?"

He started to smile. "Yes, ma'am. I will."

I went into the bedroom and snatched up the small box of condoms I 'borrowed' from the stash I put into Aaron's locker. I paused to look at myself in the mirror over the dresser. I shook my head in amazement. I almost looked beautiful. Grinning, I came back to the living room to find Sam sprawled on the couch, my afghan draped over him. He patted the edge of the seat. "Why don't you come over here and keep me warm."

I walked slowly across the room and held up the box of condoms. "I've got a four-pack," I said. "Think that'll do?"

"For starters." He raised the afghan and I saw his erection, large and red and ready to go.

I grinned. "No Viagra for you?" I asked as I slipped onto the couch next to him and he covered me with the soft afghan.

"Not with you in the same room." He watched as I opened the box and extracted a small foil packet. "Will you do the honors?"

"I'd love to." I opened the condom package and held it up. "Shall we?"

He threw back the cover and slipped his hand down to my panties, sliding them off me in one movement. "Tell me how you want it," he murmured.

I did.

****

"If I don't get out there soon, I won't have a laundry room left," I murmured a long time later.

Sam laughed, his breath hot on my neck. "I'll handle it. You stay here and keep warm." He kissed me and tossed back the afghan, bending quickly to cover me with its warm folds before striding out of the room, snagging his flannel shirt as he went and dragging it on. I enjoyed the view as he left, his little butt bouncing and his jaunty penis, sated and heavy, moving in time to his steps. I heard the murmur of his voice from the kitchen then the unmistakable sound of Houdini's enquiring 'meow?'

"Are you hungry?" Sam called from the kitchen.

I got up and ducked into the bedroom to grab a bathrobe and the chenille throw from my bed then joined Sam and Houdini in front of the fridge in the kitchen. I handed Sam the throw. "Here you go. I'd hate to have your manly parts get cold."

"I don't think that's a problem with you around," he said but he wrapped the blanket around him like a long skirt as he peered into the fridge.

"I've got some breakfast quiches I can heat up," I said, pulling out the container with my little muffin-y morsels. "Sound okay?"

Sam looked doubtfully at the plastic carton in my hand. "Quiche? You know what they say. Real men don't eat quiche."

"You'll like these," I assured him. I set five of the quiche-muffins on a plate and popped it into the microwave then turned to the coffee pot. "Coffee or wine?" I asked, looking at the clock above the sink. It was almost seven o'clock.

Sam followed my gaze. "Depends on if I'm staying the night." He put his arms around me and nuzzled my neck. "If I'm staying the night, some coffee might be useful to keep me up." He kissed me on the cheek. "Unless you can think of something else to keep me up. Man, that does smell good. I know you're a great singer and I know you're an excellent dancer. Can you cook, too?"

I turned my head slightly to meet his lips in a quick kiss. "How do you know I'm a good dancer? You've never seen me dance."

He pushed against my butt, his hips rubbing against me and leaving no doubt about his interest. "You do the horizontal rumba pretty damn good."

The microwave dinged and I disentangled myself from Sam's embrace. "You grab the wine and I'll get the food," I directed. We were soon seated at my small dining table with the breakfast quiches, grapes, a loaf of bread and wine set out in candlelight. Houdini feasted between us, a small quiche crumbled for him on a saucer on the floor.

"These are great," Sam mumbled around a bite

of quiche.

"I make them all the time," I said. "They're easy to carry to work and they last just about forever." I washed down a cheesy bite with some tart wine. It felt good to sit there with him. It reminded me of what I missed when I wasn't in a relationship—the simple companionship.

Sam finished his portion and sat back, twirling the liquid in his glass. "Have you recovered from the kiss your ex-husband gave you as he was leaving?" He tilted his head back and took a long swallow of wine.

I almost choked on my last bite of quiche. "You saw it?"

Sam nodded, nudging Houdini with his foot. My cat promptly lay down and presented his tummy for a rub. "Do you believe me now?" Sam leaned over to oblige the feline but his eyes remained on me, evaluating my reaction.

I stalled for time, getting up for a refill on my wine. When I sat back down, I said, "I don't know, Sam. Charlie and I..." I took a gulp, trying to order my thoughts. "We've always been together. We dated all through high school and college. I mean, we dated other people because Charlie went away to Harvard while I stayed here. But whenever he came home, we were together." I shook my head. "We've always been together."

Sam took my hand and ran his fingers over my rough cuticles. "I can see how it's all tangled up in your mind." He tilted his head to one side. "Who asked for the divorce?"

"It was mutual. We came to the conclusion we were better friends than we were lovers."

Sam's fingers tightened on mine. "Who asked for the divorce?"

"Charlie," I whispered.

Sam nodded. "He knew. He knew you weren't in

love with him. He knew it was the wrong thing to do."

"Are you speaking from experience?" The words slipped out before I could stop them.

He slowly removed his hand from mine. "No. Sheila and I never really connected the way you and Charlie did. We got married for the wrong reasons and stayed married for the wrong reasons. I was almost relieved when she took up with Mike. It made it easy to ask for a divorce." His voice was steady but I thought I heard residual hurt in it, even after all the years. "It was an interesting comment he made earlier, about the money."

I stared at him blankly. "Money?"

"Charlie said something like 'now money won't have to be an issue for you.' He said it when he talked about your inheritance?" Sam regarded me with alert curiosity, his dark eyes assessing. "Was it an issue for you before?"

I frowned. "No. Not really."

"Not really?" He sipped some more wine. "How much money are we talking about?"

I avoided his gaze by bending over to rub Houdi's belly. "A lot."

"Maybe that's why she did it."

My head jerked up so fast I almost decapitated myself. "What?"

"The old lady. Maybe she left you the money because she knew your lack of money bugged you. Maybe she decided to remove that impediment."

I stared at him in open-mouthed surprise. The minute he said the words, I knew he was right. How did Sam Barlow, who barely knew the Whittingtons or me, so precisely nail what was a thorny issue all these years? And how did he know what Grandy Theo, that perceptive, intelligent old woman, did for me?

"So nobody in the family ever accused you of

being a gold-digger?" he persisted.

I thought of some of the hateful things John threw at me years ago when Charlie and I got married. "It didn't matter," I said, taking his dish and mine and going to the sink. "It was a long time ago."

"Does it still hurt?" he asked softly.

I turned on the water and rinsed the dishes before putting them into the dishwasher. As I did the phone rang. I grabbed the receiver, glad for the interruption. It was Aaron again.

"I did what you suggested I do," he said breathlessly, as though afraid I'd cut him off.

"You did?" I eyed Sam, who sipped his wine while watching me with unnerving alertness. I suddenly remembered I hadn't even told Aaron who put the condoms in his locker. "Listen," I said, turning away and drifting toward the living room, away from prying ears, "I put a box in your locker earlier, at the nursery."

"Yeah, I saw it, thanks." He sounded so dismissive I wondered if he even looked in the box. Before I could ask, he hurried on, his words tumbling over each other. "I tried to talk to her about it all but she didn't want to hear it."

He sounded desperate. I went into my den to sort through my CDs, looking for a new mix to load into the player. "Aaron, I apologize, but I don't understand what your problem is. Can you be more specific? I'd like to help, really I would, but I don't understand what's going on."

"I can't tell you." His voice faded slightly as though he was on a cell phone and it was going out of range then it came back surprisingly strong. "I think I should talk to the police."

"If you think you should, then you probably should," I agreed. I reached up to grab a CD off the bookshelf and the phone dropped out of my hand.

"Sorry," I said when I'd retrieved it.

No one replied. "Aaron?"

No answer. He must have hung up. I changed out the mix of CDs and went back to the kitchen. Just as I entered, the phone in my hand rang again. "Sorry," I mumbled to Sam. "I'm normally not this popular."

"Oh, I don't believe that," he said with a laugh.

"Cassie, this is Mary Hannon. I'm sorry to bother you and I don't know if you can help me or not, but have you heard from Sam by any chance?"

I blinked in surprise. "Uh, yeah. Why?"

"I'm trying to get in touch with him and his cell phone is off and nobody answers at his apartment. I need to find him."

"Hang on." I held out the phone to Sam. "I guess the word is out. It's your sister."

"Mary? What the hell?" He took the phone. "What's up, Mary?" He listened for a minute. "Yeah, the cell phone died, I need to get a charger." Another pause then Sam's eyes went to me and he smiled. "No problem. We're just talking." He winked then listened intently for a long minute. As I watched, his face changed, taking on a tense, focused look. He stood and started walking toward the living room, the phone pressed to his ear and my bed-throw dragging behind him, unnoticed. "I'll be there in a minute. Okay."

He handed me the phone and strode to his clothing, most of it tossed on the floor near the couch. "What's wrong?" I asked as he started getting dressed.

"There's a problem at the nursery," he said tightly.

I looked at my front door as though I could see beyond it to the store just a mile away. Sam saw my look and shook his head. "At the production nursery in Jordan, south of here. Somebody broke the panes

154

of glass on the Number Three greenhouse."

I thought frantically back to my brief tour of the Barlow production greenhouses. What was in Number Three?

Sam saw my confusion. "Petunias, impatiens, and other annuals."

"Damn. Did they get frost last night?"

"I'm not sure. If they did, it's bad." He jammed his feet into his boots and bent to lace them. "We could be out a lot of money if there's frost damage."

"Let me know if I can help," I said.

He walked to the door and I fell into step with him. "Thanks, Cassie. I'll be back, if you'll let me."

I kissed him quickly. "Of course I will. And I mean it. Let me know if I can help."

He nodded then paused at the front door. "Grab the escape artist," he warned.

I looked down at my yellow cat, poised to make a leap into the unknown. "You little goof." I grabbed him up and managed to kiss Sam over the head of the wiggling body in my arms. "Call me later?"

"I'll try." Sam stared at me for a long minute then turned away. "Good night, Cassie."

I closed the door and went into the den to watch as he drove away. It looked like the campaign to put Barlow out of business was escalating.

Chapter 14

After my chaotic Saturday, my Sunday was like an oasis of calm. I slept late then went for a long walk in the warm spring morning, trying to put distance between my problems and my brain.

It didn't work, of course. My thoughts kept returning to Sam, Charlie, and Kathleen, bouncing between the amazing kiss with Charlie to the very satisfying but way too brief loving with Sam. He was passionate, fun, and oh-so-expert. My body was still on fire from his ministrations.

Also playing on the edges of my mind was the knowledge I now had Money with a capital "M". Charlie was right. The money changed everything. It wasn't just freedom from worry. It was a fundamental change to *me*. I had been self-sufficient all my life because of my hard work. Now I didn't have to work, I didn't have to worry. It changed everything.

What was I going to do? Worries seemed to pile up, dogging my feet as I walked briskly through my new neighborhood and admired the shoots of green and the emerging buds on trees while piles of snow still lurked in the shadows like vagrants. Years ago I responded to stress by eating, which was how my weight ballooned out of control. Now I responded by exercising and creating a mental Shit To Do list, sorting my problems into piles where I could manage them more easily.

The Money went into a "deal with it tomorrow" pile. I would talk to the financial people and make some decisions about my future then. One problem down and how many to go?

The Man Problem. I had an abundance of men in my life and I didn't know what to do about it. What to do about Sam? And Charlie? I couldn't call Charlie and ask, "Are you in love with me?" And even if I could, was I prepared for his answer? What did I want? For the last twenty-five years I had lived an independent life with only an occasional man to warm my bed. Now what did I have? Summer/winter; Day/Night/; Charlie/Sam.

But did I have them? Sam didn't make any promises. As far as I knew, with him I would have an evening now and again with an occasional weekend thrown in to extend our pleasure. And Charlie...? My thoughts shied away from that topic. I decided to push it low on my STD list. Charlie was a problem that needed a lot of thought and I wasn't prepared to face it on the day after I had high-energy, toe-curling sex with a man like Sam.

Did I even want a man in my life? The thought gave me pause, both literally and physically. I stopped in my tracks and stared at the highway in the distance, my brain trying to wrap around the idea of sharing my life with someone. I wasn't accustomed to compromising because of someone. My marriage to Charlie had been brief and so long ago that it was faded into memory. The few memories I did have were largely pleasant except for the ending, when we talked and cried together, trying to decide what to do.

Did I want to go through that again?

My thoughts turned to Sheila Peavey, who had a husband so suddenly taken from her. She would have to learn all over again how to live alone, how to handle things on her own. Widowhood must be a shock. My divorce crept up on me but I knew it was coming. What would it be like to become a widow because of a sudden death? Worse yet, a widow because of a murder? How stunning it must be for her. I considered that as I resumed walking, my steps a bit slower than before. Of course, she didn't appear too distraught the day I saw her. If anything she seemed angry. Well, perhaps grief took people in different ways.

I realized I had given little thought to Peavey and his untimely death in the uproar of the last few days. What killed him, or, more to the point, who killed him? There wasn't much time between when I exited the greenhouse and Sam exited the greenhouse. It was just a matter of minutes until his body was found. Who could have gone into the greenhouse and accosted him? And if Sam was right, did someone poison Peavey ahead of time? Was the blood I saw an indication of means of death or did something else kill him?

I reached the one-mile mark on my pedometer and turned to head for home, letting my mind roam freely over all the tiny facts, impressions, and random images building up for days. Some little niggling idea was trying to struggle to the surface, but whenever I tried to focus on it, the thought vanished, replaced by thoughts of Charlie or Sam. I finally gave up and simply enjoyed the day, reveling in warm sunlight, gentle breezes, and the sight of snow melting in messy rivulets from the big gray piles on the sides of the roads. Easter was just around the corner and after it would be spring, a brief explosion of growth and joy in Minnesota, a place where all seasons except winter were truncated. I was itching to start working on my little patch of soil and put my newly found horticultural knowledge to work.

Gardening brought my thoughts back to school and when I got home I decided to focus on the one thing I was sure about—final exams. I settled on the couch in the living room but I had too many memories of Sam there. I went to the den, but it felt like my walls were closing in on me. With a resigned sigh I packed up my books and headed to the Pickaway library where I spread out my papers on a table in the window-filled reference section. I resolutely pushed aside all romantic musings and turned my thoughts to pesticides and plant propagation.

Two hours after sitting down I took a break, walking around the small building with Latin names rattling around in my brain and legal mumbo-jumbo about pesticide application repeating like a litany in my mind. I turned on my cell phone and it bounced to voice mail. Livvie had left me a breathless message, asking me to call her as soon as possible. I went to one of the small study rooms where I could close the door for privacy but still see my books spread out on the wooden table. I dialed Livvie's number and she answered on the first ring.

"Cassie, what the hell is going on with Charlie?" she demanded as soon as I identified myself. "He called me last night. I think he was drinking. He said you're in love with a guy and he thinks the guy is wrong for you. So who's the man in your life?"

"He said what?"

"Come on, who's the guy? Charlie said it's some farmer or something?"

I heard the sound of ice on glass and knew Livvie was tippling again. I glanced at the clock over the front desk. It was two in the afternoon. She was probably having a Sunday afternoon Bloody Mary. I wished I could join her. "Sam's not a farmer, he owns a nursery."

"A what? You mean a baby place?"

"A landscape center and a nursery."

"Oh, good. No offense, Cassie, but you're not the baby type. So are you serious with the guy or is it just sex? It must be serious," she barreled ahead. "Otherwise Charlie wouldn't be upset. He only gets upset when you get serious about somebody."

"What?" My stomach started to twist into knots.

"I warned him this would happen. When you got divorced, I told him he was going to have to watch you fall in love with someone else. I knew this would happen someday. I have to admit, I thought it would happen a lot sooner, but I knew it would happen."

"What would happen?" My hand was sweating so much on the phone I could barely grip it, but I kept it pressed against my ear, struggling to hear her through a bad connection.

"I knew you'd go off with someone else. You're too good a catch to be left alone for your whole life. Charlie sounded worried last night, Cassie. He made it sound like this guy was putting you in danger. Are you sure you should be seeing this Sam guy? Is he after you for your money?" Livvie laughed bitterly and I heard the telltale sound of ice again as she probably sipped her drink. "I can spot a money sniffer a mile away. Do you want me to check the guy out and make sure he'd not after you for the wrong reasons?"

"I just got the money, Livvie. I met Sam before he knew I was going to get any. So I don't think he's after me for my cash." I hesitated, not sure I wanted an answer to my next question but knowing I had to ask it. "Do you think Charlie is still in love with me?" I could barely get the words out.

There was a long pause and one more telltale

rattle of ice. "I don't know," she finally said." I know he *thinks* he's in love with you. So I guess that's the same thing, isn't it?"

"Damn." I leaned forward, my elbows resting on my knees. The phone sputtered and I jerked upright, making a mental note on my STD list to find a new cell phone provider and *soon*. "I didn't think he felt that way."

"Charlie's at an awkward age," Livvie said with sisterly frankness.

"You make him sound like a teenager with a crush on his teacher." I thought fleetingly of the recent news story about the schoolteacher who lusted after her pupil. "Charlie's a grownup."

"Yeah, but he's starting to worry about old age. He's starting to worry if he's still got what it takes to attract a woman."

I almost howled. "He's the handsomest man I've ever met, for cryin' out loud."

"Charlie doesn't think in those terms."

I leaned back, my head pounding. She was right. Charlie always discounted his looks, his money, and his charm. It was one of his most endearing traits and one that struck most people as ingenuous until they got to know him better and realized it wasn't an act.

"Give him a call, Cassie. He's worried about you."

"There's nothing to worry about."

"So you think this Sam guy is on the up and up? Is it serious?"

"I have no idea, Livvie. We'll see what works out." I stood up, suddenly claustrophobic and anxious for movement. "I have to go now."

"Call Charlie, okay? And Cassie..."

"What?"

"I'm the last person to be giving advice about love." She gave another bitter snort of laughter and I winced. Livvie's marriage had appeared happy but I knew otherwise. Her husband's death eight years earlier was a relief. "Don't let Charlie's feelings interfere with your happiness. You'll always be a member of the family. You know you will, don't you?" She paused then rushed on. "It doesn't matter if you're divorced from Charlie. You're still family."

Tears burned hot in my eyes. "I know," I whispered. "I'll talk to you later, Livvie." I folded the phone and stumbled out of the little room, sinking down at the table and putting my head in my hands.

So much for my plan to postpone Charlie to the bottom of the STD list. He just bubbled back to the top. I bundled up my books and decided to go home and call him from there. At least at the townhouse I had a reliable phone connection.

I drove by Barlow's on my way but didn't see Sam's SUV in the parking lot. On impulse I pulled in and hurried into the store. Bev was manning the checkout counter and I waited for a customer to leave before asking her, "Have you talked to Mary today? I heard there was damage at the production greenhouses yesterday."

Bev nodded, her hazel eyes reflecting her anxiety. "She went out there this morning after we opened. She said they lost almost everything in the Three Greenhouse and there was also damage to Number Two. Tulips," she said with a sad nod.

"Oh, man, that's hard." I looked at the back door as it opened and Don came in. "Do they know what caused the damage?"

"Vandals," Don said. "Did you come in to help out?"

I shook my head. "I'm not slated to work again until later in the week. Why, are you short-handed?"

"Aaron didn't show up for work today," he said, his voice clearly reflecting his opinion of this dereliction of duty.

"We're not that busy," Bev said soothingly. "Aaron's probably studying for finals. Or maybe he's sick."

"He should have called in." Don went to help a customer who was eyeing the pre-emergent herbicides with a perplexed look.

"Do you need help?" I asked Bev in a low voice. "I can stay if you do."

"No, we're not that busy. And it's Sunday so we close in a couple of hours anyway. But if you talk to Aaron at school tomorrow, tell him to call Mary and explain why he was gone. She was pretty stressed out today when she found out we'd be short-handed. She didn't need that kind of worry on top of what happened at the production greenhouses."

I nodded my understanding and left before I could be put to work. As I drove the short distance home, I wondered if Barlow's could recover from the loss of two greenhouses. That probably explained why Sam didn't call. He was probably busy assessing the damage and talking to insurance people.

At least I hoped that was why he didn't call. I had a brief burst of adolescent worry (*why isn't he calling me? Doesn't he like me? Should I call him?*) but I ruthlessly pushed it aside. The man was busy and so was I. We had one night of fun and made no commitments to each other. It did no good to sweat over his communication skills.

I spent the evening practicing what I would say to Charlie when I called him but all my practice proved futile because when I finally dialed his number, he wasn't home. I chickened out and didn't leave a message and was angry at how relieved I felt because he was gone.

I had a tough struggle with my old habits and almost drove to the nearby convenience store for a pint of Rocky Road. I satisfied my craving with an Atkins shake and went to sleep triumphant over

163

calories—and lonely. For a woman who supposedly had an abundance of men, my bed was cold and empty.

I got up early on Monday and dressed with care for my lawyer appointment later in the afternoon. I still put comfort over fashion, though, and chose my newest blue jeans and a nice pastel sweater over a pale yellow turtleneck. Then I put in some last minute studying before going to school for my nine a.m. test, my brain stuffed full of pesticide application laws and diagrams.

Because it was a state-regulated test, the rules were stricter than for our regular horticultural classes. All students taking the test were assigned seats in a classroom and informed we were there for two hours. Whether we finished early or not, we had to stay in our seats. This elicited a last-minute flurry of activity as people dashed out to refill water bottles and hit the bathroom one last time.

There were only a dozen of us taking the test because only those going into nursery operations would need a commercial pesticide applicator license. I took the bulky sheaf of papers from the state proctor and lined up my number-2 pencils in a tidy row. Then I took a deep breath and embarked on my three-hundred-question, multiple-choice hell.

I was lucky time was limited, because I didn't have a chance to second-guess my answers. I went through the test in one pass and answered everything I was certain of, then went back and agonized over the ones I left blank. That left me twenty minutes to glance through everything and wonder if my mind was playing tricks on me: should the answer be A or D? Or was it "None of the above"? I resisted the urge to modify several responses and turned in my answer sheet feeling relatively certain I passed, although probably not with flying colors.

I didn't have time to savor my freedom. I dashed

to my locker to stash one set of books and grab another then headed for the cafeteria, where I had thirty minutes to eat lunch, review plant propagation, and get ready for my next test.

I looked for Aaron, but didn't see him among the milling students in the commons area outside the small cafeteria. I asked Barb if she'd seen him. "Nope," she said. "He missed the Woody Plants final. Is he sick?"

"I don't know. Save me a seat." I went into the cafeteria and got a salad then came out to join Barb and Mary Ellen, who were worrying over their performance in the Woody final.

"I'm terrible at plant identification," Mary Ellen said as she gulped down a ham sandwich. "How often will it be needed anyway? I mean, how many times does a customer find a plant and say, 'oh, this plant must be a *Fagus grandifolia* because it has ovate leaves that are broad-cuneate at the base and has monoecious flowers?' More likely somebody will see a plant and say, 'hey, I like the light brown tree-looking one, over there.' That's more practical, not all the Latin identifying marks."

I gave her a sympathetic look. I had struggled through all three Woody classes. The finals were murder because you went in a room to look at dozens of small branches lined up on tables. You then had to identify the tree it came from based on the sample. I squeaked by with "C" grades in all the classes and was happy for those grades. "Aaron didn't show up for work yesterday," I said as I shoveled the salad into my mouth.

"He must be sick," Barb said. I was surprised at her calmness. Normally she was a bundle of nerves but today, in the face of final exams, she was an oasis of placidity. "He can't make up the Woody final. At least, that's what we were told. He'll have to do extra credit if he wants to pass the class." She looked around at the students nearby then said in a low voice, "I saw Aaron with a woman yesterday."

"A woman?" I asked around a mouthful of lettuce and hot-house tomato. "Where?"

"It was outside Southview Mall, in the parking lot. It was after the mall closed. I was using the ring road around the mall to go to the movie theater and they were in one of the parking lots, out by the main highway."

I visualized the scene in my mind. Southview was a small suburban mall surrounded by a main parking lot. Smaller 'sub-lots' were farther out on its periphery, often used only at Christmastime when the mall and the main lots were clogged with people. Those sub-lots were also used for snow dumping during times of heavy accumulation and were often the last bastion of melting snirt during spring.

"I recognized him right away," she continued. "It was one of those flukes. My headlights illuminated him just right. I could barely see her, though. She was standing with her back to the road next to a red car with the door open."

"It must be the mysterious girlfriend," I said, finishing the last of my salad and gathering up my books.

"Maybe," Barb said doubtfully, picking up her books, too. "She looked older. Like a woman, not a girl, if you know what I mean."

"Maybe he was helping someone with her car," Mary Ellen suggested.

"It looked like they were arguing," Barb said as we headed toward the classrooms and our next test. "He looked upset. In fact, Bob thought we should stop. He thought they looked..." Barb shrugged. "I don't know, like something was wrong. We didn't stop, though. I told him it was none of our business."

"It was probably nothing," I said, my thoughts already turning to the task ahead. "How come you're so calm about these tests?"

"I've got an A going into finals," she said confidently. "I can get a C on these tests and still do fine."

"Lucky you," Mary Ellen muttered.

"I worked like a dog all semester so I could relax now," Barb continued blithely.

She was right but it still rankled. Mary Ellen and I exchanged exasperated looks and followed Barb into the classroom where Ed Jenkins, our instructor, awaited us with test booklets in hand.

I was more self-assured on this test because it had a mix of questions with essay, multiple-choice and matching sprinkled throughout the twelve-page exam. I finished with time to spare and left with a murmured, 'see you tomorrow' to Ed, since I had one more test with him on Tuesday. Then I raced for my locker and grabbed my coat and books.

As I did, a note fell out of the small vent at the top of the metal locker door. I stuffed it into my pocket and ran out to the Jeep, tossing my gear into the back seat for the thirty-minute drive to Minneapolis and the appointment with the lawyers to discuss the Money with the capital M that I inherited.

As I sat in the waiting room of the elegant office in a downtown skyscraper, I unfolded the note. It was from Aaron: *I've been sick but I have to go to the funeral tomorrow. I'll meet you at two outside school. Aaron.*

I completely forgot about Peavey's funeral and my promise to go with Aaron. Damn. I considered canceling it then realized I didn't have Aaron's phone number or any other way to get in touch with him. I could probably get it from Mary, but I didn't want to draw attention to him if I could help it. Nope. I was stuck.

The woman lawyer from Saturday's reading of

the will came out of an inner office, smiling at me. "I'm Janelle Rimes, Mrs. Whittington. We met on Saturday. I'm not sure if you remember. If you'll just come this way," she said, sashaying in front of me down a carpeted hallway. Today she wore navy slacks and a pink blouse under a navy jacket. Her dark hair was loosely tied back and clipped with a blue barrette, giving her a more youthful, less businesslike look.

"It's Ms. Whittington, actually," I corrected.

"Sorry. I know some women still retain the title even though they're divorced."

"Title?" I almost laughed. "Odd way to phrase it."

Her cheeks got pink. "Salutation. Since you have the same last name, I just assumed..." She cleared her throat.

I barely noticed her on Saturday, but something in her confident way of walking made me ask, "Are you a partner here?"

"Junior partner." She glanced back at me. "Mr. Whittington and I have worked together for several years. I admire his work greatly."

The warmth in her voice told me she might admire Charlie's other qualities as well. I examined her more closely. She had a thin, narrow face, vaguely Asian with sharp cheekbones and wide, dark eyes up-tilted at the corners. I couldn't judge her age. She looked in her thirties, which would make her fifteen years younger than Charlie, just the right age for the older-man/younger-woman scenario. "How long have you been Grandy—Mrs. Penningford's—lawyer?"

"Charlie recommended me six years ago. I'm grateful to him and to her. Having his grandmother as a client taught me a lot."

I grinned. "I can imagine."

She opened a door and gestured me to precede

her into a long conference room in the corner of the building, with windows on two of the walls. Two unknown men were seated on the far side of the table. John Whittington turned to glare at me from his seat near the door while the man next to him continued studying the papers on the table in front of him.

Charlie looked up from his spot at the head of the conference room table. He looked tired and somehow thinner, as though he lost weight overnight. "I didn't know you planned to be here, Charlie," I said, following the female lawyer to a spot at the opposite end of the table.

"John mentioned he was coming and I thought you might like some other family members to be here, too." He smiled at me, but his eyes were cold and assessing.

I understood immediately what he wasn't saying. John was getting ready to pitch a fit and Charlie was there to back me up, regardless of how he felt. It looked like I had a fight ahead of me. I took a deep breath and sat down in the plush leather chair.

Chapter 15

"Mrs. Whittington, we're here to discuss the disposition of Mrs. Penningford's estate," a distinguished looking man said from his seat at the table opposite John. "I'm Mark Colton and this is Mr. Anderson, an associate with our firm. We acted as attorneys for Mrs. Penningford when she was alive." His tone of voice told me this was an impressive accomplishment.

"It's Ms. Whittington," I corrected. "And I was under the impression Ms. Rimes was the primary attorney for Mrs. Penningford."

Colton looked uncomfortable. "Ms. Rimes was primary attorney, but—well, now that Mrs. Penningford is dead, you may decide you want the full range of our client services at your disposal." He said this blandly, as though he hadn't just insulted the woman sitting next to me. Charlie shot him a disgusted look but didn't say anything.

"We'll see," I murmured. My gaze skimmed over the impassive man next to Colton and settled on John and the man next to him. "And you, John?" I asked quietly. "Why are you here?"

For answer, the man next to him slid a business

card across the table to me. I glanced at it, confirming what I suspected. Another lawyer. "I'm representing the Whittington family," the man said.

"Some of the family," Charlie snapped frostily. He looked at Colton. "Let's continue."

Janelle Rimes handed me a sheaf of papers in a leather binder. She appeared calm and composed in the face of a senior lawyer's dismissal of her, but I saw her fingers tremble. Her cuticles were a bit ragged with telltale red spots where she probably picked at the skin. The sight gave me an instant feeling of sisterly understanding since I had the same bad habit.

"This is a complete listing of Mrs. Penningford's holdings." Her eyes went to Charlie, who regarded us with an impassive stare as though we were two strangers who drifted in and sat down at his conference table. I returned his impassivity with a stare of my own and he broke eye contact, shifting his gaze to Colton and his minion.

Colton kicked off the talk by directing me to page one of the report in front of me. We droned through page after page of mutual funds, bonds, investments, real estate, and personal possessions. I made an occasional note in the spiral notebook I brought with me for that purpose but I was more interested in the interpersonal byplays going on in the conference room than I was in the Money. I'd have to read all the paperwork later anyway, so I allowed the words to wash over me as I watched Charlie and the way he avoided looking at Janelle Rimes.

Was it my imagination? Ms. Rimes and I were sitting directly opposite Charlie at the end of the conference table. All he had to do was raise his head and look at her. But he kept his eyes either on Colton or on the painting over my right shoulder.

And Janelle Rimes? She was doing the same

thing, although without as much success. She kept her eyes focused on Colton but her gaze kept shifting to Charlie. Whenever it did, her cheeks got flushed or she fiddled with her pencil or shifted in her chair. Granted, Charlie was the handsomest man in the room, but her reaction to his presence was surprising.

"Do you have any questions, Mrs. Whittington?"

I looked down at the doodles I made in the notebook. "I'll correct you one more time," I said slowly. "It's Ms. Whittington. Charlie and I are divorced."

Colton sat back, obviously surprised by my cold tone. "I apologize." He looked at Charlie, as though unsure of his reaction, but Charlie's calm, impersonal expression didn't waver. "Are there any questions?"

"Yes," I said, looking at John. "What makes you angrier? That she gave me the money or that she gave you so little?"

Colton said, "Uh, Mrs.—Ms.—Whittington, I don't believe you will be comfortable discussing personal matters..."

His voice trailed away when I turned my head slowly to regard him. "I'm very comfortable discussing this." I turned my attention back to John, my expression polite.

John's eyes, so like Charlie's, narrowed with anger. I didn't think he was going to say anything then he suddenly spat, "Your father killed my mother. How could she forgive you? How could she reward you? It was her only daughter. She gave money to the daughter of the man who murdered her only child."

Janelle Rimes sucked in a shocked breath and Colton sat up straighter, obviously surprised. Either Grandy Theo hadn't told them about the family's sordid past or they all thought it was done and buried. I knew it wasn't. I knew we had to air this dirty little bit of family laundry before we could get down to what was really festering in John and making him so bitter.

"I asked her about it once," I said, keeping my gaze steadily on John, who glared at me with such hatred it twisted my guts. "I know it was my fault. My mother would have left town if not for me. But she couldn't run far with a child in tow and she had to take your mother's help, she had to do what she could to protect me. So it was my fault." I shot Charlie a quelling look when he started to speak. "It was. I asked Grandy Theo how she could stand to be with me. I asked her how she could forgive me."

"There was nothing to forgive," Janelle whispered next to me.

I looked at her in surprise. "That's what she said to me. Did she talk about it?"

Janelle nodded then she stared at Charlie, who stood and walked to the window, his shoulders hunched as he stared out at the city. She followed him with her eyes, which were sad and perplexed. "We were all talking about it one day. Mr. Whittington, Mrs. Penningford and me. We were at her house and discussing the estate. I asked her the same thing. I didn't understand how she could stand to have the two people around her who were directly responsible for her daughter's death. I couldn't understand how..." Her cheeks turned a dark red but she continued doggedly on, "I couldn't understand how a member of the family could marry you after what happened."

"Mr. Whittington?" I looked at Charlie. "Do you mean Charlie or his father?"

He glanced at me over his shoulder. "Me."

"Ah." Little puzzle pieces started dropping into place, but the picture was still incomplete. I decided to pursue that mystery later and deal with John instead. I turned my attention to him. "Grandy told me that my mother did what any mother would do, what your mother would have done in the same circumstance. She protected her child. There was nothing to forgive. Grandy said she was honoring her daughter's memory by helping me and loving me. It would be too easy to blame my mother and me. Grandy Theo would never take the easy way out."

Janelle took a deep, ragged breath next to me. "She loved you very much. She felt you needed the money more than the others and such a bequest could benefit you more than the others."

"And she was right," Charlie said in a low, angry voice while still staring out the window at downtown Minneapolis. "The will is crystal clear and you can't fight it, John. Cassie gets the money and there's nothing you can do."

John started to speak but I overrode him. "I've decided how I'd like to dispose of Grandy's estate."

You could have heard a pin drop in the room. Charlie turned around to stare at me. "What do you mean, 'dispose of the estate?'"

I ignored him and looked at Janelle. "I'm counting on you to help me figure this all out." She nodded but looked worried. I smiled reassuringly. "I'm going to take one-third of the money to set up the Gloria Penningford Whittington Foundation, to assist women to leave abusive relationships. I want John's oldest son and Becky's oldest daughter to serve on the board of directors and help me get it set up. I think it's crucial the family be involved in the foundation." I didn't wait for their reaction but continued, anxious to get the words out while my courage still supported me.

"I want to use another one-third of the inheritance for various charitable contributions. The remainder is money I'll invest and use to supplement my income." I met Charlie's angry stare. "My income from my job at Barlow's Nursery."

"Trying to make your conscience clearer?" John demanded.

I met his gaze squarely. "Yes."

My answer seemed to shame him. He looked from me to Charlie. "Are you going to let her do this?"

"Charlie has nothing to do with it. It's my decision." Charlie and I locked gazes. "Charlie has nothing to do with this," I repeated softly.

John stood up abruptly. "This isn't the end of it, Cassie. You can't buy your way out by offering my son a spot on some mythical board of directors." He turned and left the room, his surprised lawyer trailing behind him.

I watched them go then turned my attention to Charlie, who still stared at me. I realized I was afraid to speak the next words, but I knew I had to say them. "It's time to let go, Charlie. It's time to move on."

The brief hurt in his eyes was quickly replaced by a businesslike, calm mask. "Of course. You can do what you want to with the money, Cassie." His glance moved to Janelle. "I'm sure Miss Rimes can help you. Now if you'll excuse me, I was going to look into that contract dispute for Sam Barlow." His lips twisted in a wry smile. "Business before pleasure." He nodded once to Colton then left the room, leaving behind a stunned silence in his wake.

I smiled weakly at Colton. "Family squabble," I said in what I hoped was a casual voice. "It happens all the time with the Whittingtons. I appreciate you taking the time to discuss the estate with me. I'm sure Miss Rimes and I can work out the details of what needs to be done."

He recognized my tone of dismissal but refused to give away command of the situation completely.

"Does this mean you plan to retain our firm to handle your affairs? You plan to continue the relationship Mrs. Penningford set up?"

"As long as Miss Rimes is willing to work with me," I said with a glance at the woman next to me.

She seemed frozen with shock but my words awakened her from her trance. "Of course I'll continue," she said faintly. "Shall we discuss some of the details now or do you need to leave?"

"We can get started now." I looked pointedly at the door and Colton took the hint, standing with his minion rising a second after him. "Thank you, gentlemen. I appreciate your time on my behalf."

I waited until the door was closed then I moved my chair so I could look directly at Janelle Rimes. "How long have you been in love with Charlie?"

****

I barely noticed the congested freeways as I drove home on autopilot, my brain befogged with too much information.

It took some digging and interpretation of innuendo on my part, but I now knew Janelle and Charlie had an affair. They were together for three years but she broke it off two years earlier. I vaguely remembered he was involved with someone back then, but we usually didn't share the details of our various relationships and I didn't pry. I remember he was upset when it ended and he had hopped from woman to woman for a while before he met Kathleen.

Janelle wouldn't tell me why they ended it, but I think I knew. It was the same reason Charlie and Kathleen broke up and their relationship didn't work.

Me.

What a fucked-up mess. I reined in my impatience on the crawling freeway, at the same time restraining my impulse to scream with frustration. Charlie and I had to talk and we had to do it *now*. We had to clear the air between us before this—whatever 'this' was—went any further.

I got home as it was getting dark, pausing to get my mail and newspaper from the box on the street. I fed Houdi then changed into old, comfortable jeans and my *Do you really want me to open my can of Whoop-Ass?* sweatshirt, which exactly matched my mood.

I skimmed the newspaper I had tossed on the bed in front of me. The capture of the Pickaway Pervert led the front page with a banner headline. The man was caught inside a house where a teenage girl was home alone. He attacked her but she managed to get away and hit the panic button on her security system, which brought the police to the house. She escaped rape but was still badly hurt.

"Thank God we don't have to worry about that anymore," I told Houdini as he escorted me to the kitchen and joined me in an inspection of the refrigerator. I glanced at the security alarm on the wall near the mudroom door and realized guiltily I once again forgot to set it. I did so before settling down with a microwave dinner in front of the television.

The news played unheard as I chewed my meal and digested the information Janelle Rimes gave me. I left half of the meal uneaten and was mentally girding my loins for a call to Charlie when my phone rang. My caller ID said, "Pickaway PD" and I answered, wondering why the police were getting in touch with me.

"Miss Whittington, this is Detective Saul Logan with the Pickaway Police Department. How are you tonight?"

Worried, upset, stressed, and nervous, I wanted to say. Instead I answered, "Fine. What's up?"

"I'm calling to tell you we recovered a piece of

property of yours. Are you missing the remote control for your garage?"

"My remote control?" I stared at the newspaper, which I carried into the dining room with me. "Yes, I am."

"We recovered it when we made an arrest last week. We traced it to you by the serial numbers on the back and the vendor name. It's here at the station if you'd like to pick it up."

"Was it..." The words clogged in my throat. "Who had it?"

There was a long pause. "Tom Stone had it in his possession when we arrested him."

I frantically peered down at the paper. *Tom Stone, age 30, arrested in a series of assaults on women in Pickaway,* the newspaper article reported. "Holy shit," I breathed. "The Pervert? Is that how he got into the houses? I suppose that's it, isn't it?"

"We're still investigating the how and why of what he did, but yes, it looks like he stole the openers from women's cars, made a note of the entry code, then returned the openers. Apparently he didn't have time to return yours."

"I'm glad I changed the code as soon as I discovered it was missing." I silently thanked an ex-lover from years ago, who once demonstrated how easy it was to break into my house using only the transmission code from my remote control. His little demo impressed me enough to remember the lesson all these years later.

"I'm glad you did, too. You might have become a victim like the others."

I remembered the pickup truck sitting on the street by the nursery and shivered. Had it been this Tom Stone creep, waiting to pounce? "No kidding."

"You can stop at the station to get the opener. You'll just need to fill out a couple of forms."

I promised to drop by later in the week and

hung up the phone, going immediately to my security gadget and checking to make sure it was properly armed. Then I flopped on the couch in the living room, stunned by my near miss with a Really Bad Guy.

The couch reminded me of Sam. I bounded to my feet and went to the den, turning on the computer and loading up the CD changer with some greatest hits compilations. I saw my notepad on the desk with my 'list of things to buy' and added 'phone for den' to the list. Then I addressed my email queue, answering a couple from the ELLs about lunch on the morrow and checking my SPAM bucket for anything that may have been diverted by mistake.

Hot nights are guaranteed with well hung dudes. "No kidding," I muttered. "And if Sam was here, I'd prove it."

A big rod will win you a perfect sexual reputation!

Want to be a hero in bed?

"Oh, for cryin' out..." I scrolled through the screenful of subject lines, each more ludicrous than the next, clicking 'delete' as I went and consigning them to the 'Permanently Delete' bucket forever.

Hot chik seeks hot man with big d!ck
You're lucky 'cause you found a super pill
Bigger dick gives incomparable pleasure
Enrich your pen!s with volume and power
I was looking for you today
4 girls from our site want you!
Bigger phallus will—

My eyes drifted over the names attached to the messages. Jeanie Easy, Willie Big, Padmanda Schlong, Aaron S., Chris Long, Damian Pitts—

"Oh, shit." Aaron S? Aaron Swenson? I saw the message disappearing even as I realized the message with the *I was looking for you today* subject line was probably legitimate. I checked the Trash bucket but the message was long gone, disappeared into the ether.

"Damn it." I leaned back and glared at my unoffending computer screen. What did Aaron want? Was it about the funeral tomorrow? I gnawed on my lower lip, thinking furiously. What if he wanted to cancel? Given all the fuss going on in my life, a missed funeral would be a welcome relief. Was there any way to get the message back?

I poked around in the Trash bin on my computer, but the email was thoroughly vanished. Well, he had my phone number. If it was urgent, he'd call.

The lights from a vehicle in my drive briefly illuminated the opposite wall and I heard a door open then slam. I got up and peeked through the peephole at the front door. Sam was coming up my sidewalk, a bouquet of flowers in his hand.

I smiled at Houdini, who was, as usual, poised for a fast exit into the Unknown. "Looks like I might have a hero in my bed tonight after all."

Chapter 16

I scooped up my antsy cat and pulled open the door before Sam could knock. "Hey, stranger," I said, stepping aside so he could enter the foyer. I closed the door behind him and let Houdi slip from my arms.

"I'm glad I'm welcome," Sam said ruefully, holding out the flowers. "I should have called yesterday but I was busy. I didn't mean to—" He suddenly grinned, "—you know, eat and run like I did on Saturday."

I laughed and put my arms around him. "You were busy," I murmured into his shirtfront. "And so was I. Not a problem." Anxiety I didn't know I was feeling dropped away from me like a dark, nasty little cloud. He *did* care. He *did* like me. High school worries and self-doubt vanished. I guess no matter how old you get, the whole relationship thing never gets simpler.

Sam's arms around me were strong and tight. I leaned into his embrace, raising my face to his. Our kiss left me breathless and hanging on for dear life, the flowers drooping from my hand dangerously close to Houdi's curious nose. When Sam released me, I jerked the flowers upright. "Better get these in water," I said my body tingling from his touch. I always thought a phrase like that was some romance book cliché, but it was true. I really was tingling and in 'female' places which seldom felt tingles any more...until I met him, that is. "Come on in."

He kicked off his boots and slung his jacket onto the coat rack in the foyer then we went into the kitchen where I fussed around, cutting the flowers and arranging them in a vase. Sam took a seat at my kitchen island and watched. "I thought about getting a flower department for the Roseville store," he commented. "There isn't a florist for miles around there."

"I think it would do well if you started small. Don't try to compete with any of the big guys." I glanced over my shoulder at him. "What happened with the greenhouses out in Jordan?"

He frowned. "It's a mess. We lost about half the tulips and a third of the annuals. We were lucky, though. The panes can be easily replaced. It'll be expensive but whoever did it didn't hurt the frame, which would have been really pricey."

"Who do you think did it?" I asked.

He shrugged. "Whoever's got it in for us."

"Your ex-wife?"

"Somehow I don't see Sheila going out to the middle of a farm field in Jordan and hefting a bunch of rocks through our greenhouse roof." His tone of voice was teasing but I heard the hint of suspicion in it nonetheless.

"Maybe she has an accomplice."

"Maybe." He reached down and picked up Houdi, plopping the big cat on his lap and giving him a brisk rub. "I didn't ask before I dropped in. Do you want me here? I mean, is it okay if I stop by like this?"

He sounded worried about his reception, which I

suppose made sense given how odd our relationship had started. I put the flowers on the counter and leaned across it to stare into Sam's eyes. "Yes." I shook a finger at him. "But next time call ahead, okay?" I looked down at my worn clothing. "Sometime you might want to see me dressed up." He looked so relieved I grinned. "What? You thought I'd kick you out?"

He let the cat slip to the floor and came around the island to take me in his arms. "I wasn't sure," he whispered. "I'm a bit out of practice with the man-woman thing." He nudged me with his pelvis and I wrapped my arms around his neck.

"You feel in practice to me."

"If I recall, you mentioned a bed the other day," he murmured as his lips came close to mine. "I was thinking we might want to explore that possibility."

I snagged the Wine in a Box and gestured toward the kitchen cupboard. "You grab the glasses and follow me."

"Your wish is my command," he said, turning to the glassware.

I laughed. "I'm counting on it."

****

An hour or so later I stirred in Sam's arms as the phone rang in the living room. "I think I'll let the answering machine get it," I said languidly. I was bruised, loved, and wrung out from a lot of sex and more than one orgasm. I hadn't felt this good in a long, long time.

Sam sighed happily. "Did I mention I'm glad I met you?"

"The feeling's mutual." I ran a hand over his chest and snuggled against him, happy for his warmth as the sweat from our bodies cooled in the chill spring air. I had the nearby window cracked slightly and could smell the moist scent of earth outside, wafted into the room on a gentle west breeze. The setting sun warmed the room but the air held a hint of coolness, making Sam's nearness comfortable. "I'm still worried about the other employees," I said, voicing what had been bugging me for days. "I don't care what you say, Sam. I'm sleeping with the boss."

"We haven't slept yet," he pointed out, pulling me closer to him.

"You know what I mean. I don't want the others to—" I heard an angry voice in the distance and strained to hear. "Is that on my answering machine?"

He listened, too. "Sounds like somebody is peeved with you."

I slid out of bed and padded out to the hall, reaching into the bathroom to grab my bathrobe from the hook on the door. "It sounds like Charlie. What's his problem?" I went out into the living room and crossed the room to the phone on the small stand near the couch. There was one message on my machine. I touched the button to play it back and Charlie's angry voice filled the room.

"Damn it, Cassie, pick up the phone. We need to clear the air and we need to do it now. I can't believe you pulled that shit today at the meeting. What do you mean you're giving away ten million dollars? I know you're there, pick up the fucking phone, damn it. I want to talk to you." There was a long, angry pause. "I'm going to keep calling until you pick up the phone, so don't think you can get away with this shit." A loud, abrupt noise indicated he'd slammed the phone down.

I stared at the machine in stunned surprise. Charlie never, ever swore.

"You gave away ten million dollars?"

I whirled. Sam was standing in the doorway to the bedroom, a towel wrapped around his middle. "I haven't given it away yet," I said. "I'm planning to."

"How much money did you inherit?"

"Fifteen million, give or take some." My hand hovered over the phone then I drew it away. "Why is Charlie so upset?"

"Fifteen million?" Sam crossed his arms on his bare chest as Houdi wandered around his feet. "Give or take some? You're pretty blasé about it."

"I've had a few days to get used to the idea. Besides, I haven't seen the money yet," I pointed out. "I'm not going out and buying a Porsche or anything until I see some cash."

"What meeting is he talking about?" Sam moved into the room to stand next to me, slipping an arm around my shoulders.

I removed my hand from the vicinity of the phone. "I had a meeting with a bunch of lawyers today. We talked...oh, damn. That's it. Janelle."

"Say what?"

I took the portable phone out of the cradle and wandered over to the couch to flop down. Sam joined me, pulling me to him then tugging the afghan around both of us so we were huddled under its warmth. Houdi hopped up on the cushions behind us to better eavesdrop on our conversation. "I met one of Charlie's ex-girlfriends today," I said. "She works with him at the law firm. They were hot and heavy a few years ago then—" The phone in my hand rang. I answered it immediately. "Charlie, is that you?"

"What the hell are you thinking of, giving away all that money?"

I was sure Sam could hear Charlie's angry voice. My neighbor two doors away could probably hear. "There's no need to shout at me, I can hear you."

He modulated his tone slightly. "Grandy didn't give you the money so you could give it to charity just to appease John."

"This has got nothing to do with John," I lied. "I think I can manage to live on what I keep." Sam chuckled beside me.

"Who's with you?" Charlie demanded.

"None of your business. What's the real problem, Charlie? What's got you in such a fit?"

"You had no right to pry into Janelle's life."

I leaned back and snuggled into Sam's embrace, feeling his comforting warmth like an added blanket around me. He smelled of sweat, and sex, and man. All were aromas that were highly intoxicating and addicting. Houdi must have thought the same thing because his paw strayed to Sam's white hair, playing with the thick strands disarrayed from our activity.

"I didn't pry," I said. "I could tell she cared about you. Why didn't your relationship work out?"

"Janelle is too young for me," Charlie said quickly. "She's only thirty-five. I don't have anything in common with her."

I almost laughed out loud. "Bullshit. This isn't about age and you know it. Was it the same problem as Kathleen? Did Janelle want a commitment? I think you have a problem with commitment, Charlie." I took a deep breath and plunged into the deep end. "I think you're using me as an excuse to keep people—to keep women—at bay."

"Good point," Sam murmured, leaning forward and kissing me on the cheek.

"That's bullshit." Charlie's voice was so cold I actually shivered. "You and I were done a long time ago. It's you who can't let go, Cassie."

I straightened indignantly, leaning forward to blast Charlie through the phone. Sam pulled me back gently. "We're friends, Charlie, and that's it. I have no illusions about our relationship, but I think you do. I think you need to examine what's going on with the women in your life and figure out why you can't make a relationship work."

"Now you're prying into my life. What gives you the right?"

I laughed. "This from the man who called Livvie and complained about the guy who I'm seeing?"

'The guy' whispered, "He did what?"

"Is it him? Is Sam Barlow with you? I thought you had more sense, Cassie. Barlow doesn't care about you. He's just out for an easy—"

"Careful, Charlie," I warned, my dormant anger finally stirring. "You can pick on me but I won't let you pick on Sam. My relationship with him has nothing to do with you."

"What relationship?" There was a pause. "Did you sleep with him?"

"Everybody assumes we sleep," Sam mumbled behind me. "What the hell is it with you people? I've got better things to do with you than sleep."

Charlie's voice lowered so much I had to strain to hear. "I can't believe you were that stupid, Cassie. You know what kind of man he is. He's not going to get serious about you."

I sat upright. "I'm not as stupid as you, Charlie. At least when I got divorced, I knew it was over."

"Ouch," Sam said softly.

"Fine," Charlie snapped. "I'll send my findings to Mary Hannon tomorrow. That's why he's sleeping with you, of course. He and his sister need help with the contract problems, right?"

"Now just a damn minute," Sam said, reaching for the phone.

"Good-bye, Charlie." I pressed the 'off' button just as Sam got his hand on the receiver. I stuffed the phone into the folds of the blanket and crossed my arms on my chest. "That son of a bitch," I fumed. "How dare he?"

"No shit. What an asshole."

"What's his problem?" I popped to my feet and strode out to the kitchen then remembered the Wine in a Box was in the bedroom. I wheeled and went back to the bedroom, almost running over Sam who was headed in the same direction.

He vanished into the bathroom and I went into the bedroom to refill my wine glass and work myself into a snit. I settled back on the tumbled sheets and dragged my bedspread over my legs. What the hell was the matter with Charlie? I'd dated men before and been in long-term relationships before and he never acted this way. Why was my relationship with Sam giving him such temper tantrum?

I took a long drink of wine, suddenly remembering what Livvie said. Charlie was worried about getting old. Okay, let's say he was worried. Did he have to take it out on me? I heard the toilet flush and listened to Sam moving around in the bathroom. Charlie and Sam were the same age and Sam didn't have those issues.

What the hell was going on with Charlie?

Sam came into the room, talking to Houdini, who paced at his side. "Yeah, you're right," he said to the cat.

"About what?"

Sam dropped his towel and got into bed with me. "He said I should probably leave some sweatpants or a robe or something here. It's a lot more comfortable walking around a house partly naked instead of fully naked." He regarded me with a half-serious, half-amused look in his dark eyes. "What do you think of your cat's idea?"

I swallowed hard. "You mean, like, move in?"

"Nah. Just get comfortable." He lay down and propped his head up on his crooked elbow, running a finger down my leg where it was outlined by the bedspread. "Nothing serious."

The words jolted me. "I suppose," I said lamely.

"Don't sound so enthusiastic," Sam commented. He patted the bed and Houdi jumped up, schmoozing against his new best friend. "I heard through the grapevine the police are looking at Sheila for Mike's murder."

I was so surprised I almost dropped my wine. "What?"

Sam nodded, his dark eyes bemused. "Apparently the poison Mike was given could have been administered a few days before he died. Two days before he died he was at some fundraiser and nobody else got sick. The day before he died he was at his company most of the day. He and Sheila had dinner the same evening, but she didn't get sick. So the police started to look at other possibilities."

"But why would she kill him?" I narrowed my eyes suspiciously. "And who's this 'grapevine' you mentioned? Do you have an in with the cops or something?"

Sam laughed as Houdi butted against his arm, insisting on some attention. "You might say so. I've known Darryl Holleran most of my life. I gave him a call and pumped him for some information." He noticed my blank look. "Darryl's the Chief of Police in Pickaway. He and I went to school together."

"Ah. So you have friends in high places."

"So to speak." He petted Houdi with heavy, spine-pushing strokes. The cat responded with claws in the bedding and a rumbling purr. "Why would Sheila kill him?" Sam shrugged. "I'm not sure. I don't think she would do it for money, although Mike made a good salary." He frowned. "More than I'll ever see in a year, that's for sure." His eyes went to mine. "You inherited fifteen million dollars and you're giving most of it away?"

"Closer to eighteen," I admitted. "And yes, I'm going to set up a foundation for abused women and also establish some scholarships." I set my wine glass down on the nightstand and lay back on the bed. Houdi immediately came to me to snuggle near my head. "And I'm going to give his alma mater some money." I disentangled his paw from my hair and smiled at Sam. "The Humane Society. I think I can adequately live on what remains."

"So are you going to quit your job?" Sam asked, scooting up to lie down and face me, the sheets draped over his body.

"I haven't thought too far ahead." I ran a finger down his arm.

His dark eyes were fixed on my face. "Are you going to get back together with Charlie now that you've got money?"

I stared at him in surprise. "What?"

"It was one of the things that stood between you, right?" I opened my mouth to deny it but Sam didn't let me speak. "You hated being dependent on him for money. Well, now you won't be. Now you're equals."

I drew back slightly. "That wasn't why Charlie and I broke up."

"But it was one of the reasons, right?"

"Hell, Sam, it was a long time ago. I don't remember why we broke up. It just wasn't working out. The point is, we broke up and we're staying broke up. The money won't change anything."

"Really?"

I looked away from the insistent expression in his eyes. Who was I kidding? Of course the money would change things. I just wasn't sure how.

"So are you going to forget about us little guys when you're rich?"

My eyes snapped back to his. "What's that supposed to mean?"

Sam sat up in the bed. "It's a lot of money."

"Just come out with it, Sam, and say what you mean." I was getting tired of this cat and mouse game.

"What are you going to do about Charlie?"

"Nothing." I kept my voice even and calm.

"Wrong move, Cassie."

"Damn it, Sam, that's not fair! Charlie and I

have history."

He stared at me. "You and I have history now, too."

"So I have to choose between the two of you, is that it?"

He shook his head. "I didn't mean it that way. I guess it's not the same. We're friends, but we don't have that kind of history together."

His cavalier dismissal of our relationship, tenuous as it was, stung. "Then you have no right to be questioning me about him, do you?"

A mixture of emotion flitted across his face, one after the other: concern, anger, worry, embarrassment and, finally, bewilderment. "No, I guess not." He pushed aside the covers and got out of bed. "I need to get going. I still have a ton of crap to handle for the insurance because of the damage."

I watched him dress, a thousand words running through my brain but none coming together into anything cohesive. "Sam," I finally said as he buttoned his shirt.

He looked over his shoulder at me. "It's okay, Cassie. You're right. We're friends and I don't have any right to presume on that friendship." He smiled but it didn't reach his eyes. "Looks like I'm doing a hit and run thing again. I'm sorry. Maybe..."

Maybe what? Maybe someday he'd want to stay? I smiled, hoping it looked genuine. "It's okay. I know you're busy." I gave a fake little laugh. "And so am I. I've got a bunch of legal paperwork to work through plus I've got exams tomorrow. I need to do some last-minute studying."

He looked so relieved I wanted to cry. "Good. I mean, I know you're busy. I'll get in touch with you later on this week, maybe. Or I'll see you at the store." He smiled wryly. "No need to advertise our relationship, I guess. Maybe you're right."

I didn't want to hear any more. "No," I said,

nudging Houdi aside and getting up. "It's not important." I strode to the bathroom door.

"I didn't mean it that way," he said quietly.

"Right." I went into the bathroom and stared at myself in the mirror.

"Cassie. What I meant was I—we—we're not sure where we're going with this. If it turns out—oh, hell, I'm not saying this right. I meant—"

"I know what you meant, Sam." I forced my voice to be calm and measured. "Let's not rush into anything, declare anything. We'll just see where things go. And until we know, there's no reason to announce anything." I brushed by him and led the way into the living room toward the front door.

"Yeah, good. Let's just see..."

I tuned him out, focusing on the foyer, the door, and the fact he was leaving and I might not see him again. What did I expect? Neither of us even hinted at an emotional involvement. He was a fun guy and we had a good time. That was it. End of story. I reached the door and Sam put a hand on my arm, pulling me to him.

"I like you, Cassie. I want to be with you but I'm not sure if I'm ready to share you with Charlie. I think you have some things to resolve before you're ready to move on. I don't want to interfere with that."

I looked up at him, my hands on his chest, keeping him at bay. "You don't know anything about it, Sam. And I'm sorry you don't want to learn."

He released me slowly, his eyes studying me then he nodded. "You're probably right." He slipped on his boots and grabbed his coat from the rack. "Take care of the escape artist."

I swooped up Houdi in my arms and watched as Sam opened the door. He paused and looked back at me. "We're not done, Cassie. Not by a long shot."

I kept my face still. "Talk to you later."

Sam pulled open the door and left quickly.

I let Houdini slide out of my arms and I turned away, going back to the couch to have a nice long, relaxing cry.

Chapter 17

Having your lover walk out on you doesn't help a person's focus, as I discovered when I tried to study later that night. I stared at the page, stared into space, remembered what we said, then stared at the page again. Then I repeated it all from square one, complete with sighs and *what would have happened if...*

I finally gave up and pulled over the legal papers to study. Janelle had put together a simple list of holdings, estimated market value, and which would be best to consider for liquidation or transfer to a charitable foundation. I stared at the list of assets and figures, finally seeing the logic in her suggestions and making notes about things still confusing to me.

At midnight I set the alarm and turned in. I couldn't sleep, though. The bed smelled like Sam, a musky, male aroma that made me long to have him there. After tossing for a few minutes I got up and changed the sheets then settled back down, Houdi stretched out in his spot on my feet. I slept fitfully until dawn then got up, made coffee and tried some studying again.

I was getting dressed for the day when Mary Hannon called. "I hate to bother you, Cassie," she said apologetically. "I know it's early but have you talked to Aaron Swenson lately? He didn't come in for work on Sunday or Monday. I thought there might be a misunderstanding about his hours."

"No, I haven't, Mary." I silently blessed her for reminding me about Aaron and my promise to attend Michael Peavey's funeral with him. I pulled out my Marrying-and-Burying outfit instead of the jeans I'd planned on for the day. "Aaron wasn't in my classes that I had exams for yesterday. I've got finals in Greenhouse Ops and Nursery Ops today, though, and he should be in both. Plus he and I were going to Michael Peavey's funeral."

"Really? I didn't know you knew Mike Peavey."

"I don't. But Aaron felt he should go because Peavey worked with his father and he was nervous about attending alone, so I said I'd go with him." I laughed unconvincingly. "We're representing the school and the Horticulture Department."

"You'll probably see Sam there." Mary said this over-casually, revealing what I suspected was the true purpose of her call.

"He'll go? It might be awkward, wouldn't it? I mean, Sheila's his ex-wife." I tried to keep my voice as casual and I-don't-care as hers.

"Oh, Sam put Sheila behind him years ago. Just years. Although it's taken him a long time to learn to trust people again." She lowered her voice to a confiding tone. "You know how some men are. They're just afraid to show how they feel. They're afraid to *say* how they feel. Sam's one of those silent types. No matter how much he cares for someone, he's afraid to make the first move and say how much he cares."

I dragged on my pants, the phone jammed between my shoulder and ear. "I suppose that's why he hasn't remarried, then."

"I don't think he's met the right person," Mary said immediately. "Sam needs somebody who has the same interests, somebody who'll take the time to get to know him. He's not the most loveable person, is he?"

I considered a few replies then finally settled on, "He's a puzzle."

"Exactly." She sounded relieved. "You just can't take him at face value. Even if it seems he's being, well, casual, he probably isn't. He probably really does care a lot about...things."

I pulled the phone away as I slipped on my navy sweater. I was too tired to spar words with Mary today. I went back to the purported topic of the call and decided to consider her innuendos later, when I was less exhausted. "When I see Aaron I'll have him call in, Mary," I said. "I'm sure it's just a misunderstanding. He's such a solid kid."

"Okay, thanks." She paused then said, "I hope you'll give Sam a chance, Cassie."

I looked at myself in the mirror over my old dresser. A tired, worried woman stared back at me. "I have, Mary. We'll see what happens. I've got to go now."

"Oh. Well, good. Okay. I'll see you at work tomorrow."

"Yep. Bye." I hung up the phone and stared at myself closer. I needed some makeup and had to fix my hair if Sam was going to be at the funeral. Then I mentally laughed at myself. He'd seen me at my worst. There was no reason to primp for him. But I went into the bathroom anyway and fussed around with my meager cosmetic collection before grabbing my books and purse and heading out the door.

Matt Larson, the landscape design instructor, stopped by my locker at school as I was putting my coat away. "Have you seen Aaron Swenson? You work with him out at Barlow's, right? He missed his Design final yesterday."

"Everybody's looking for Aaron," I said worriedly. "I'm supposed to see him this afternoon. If I do, I'll tell him to get in touch with you."

"He's got a lot of work to make up," Matt said. "His attendance and his homework really took a hit this semester. Do you know if something wrong at home? Is everything okay with him? He was such a good student going into this semester."

I slammed the locker and twirled the combination lock. "I think his father had some problems at his company," I said, struggling to remember what someone told me about Aaron's father and Mike Peavey. "But I'm not aware of anything else."

Matt fell into step with me as I walked to the classroom where my Ops classes were held. "If you see him, have him contact us. We'll cut him a break if there's a problem. Aaron's always been a good student."

"Will do." I ducked into the classroom and took my usual seat with Mary Ellen and Barb, who were already seated with pencils sharpened and ready on their desk.

I spent the next three hours in Exam Mode and by noon I was a free woman. I packed up the old garden gloves, assorted papers, and half-used notebooks from my locker and walked out of the building with the ELLs who were going to lunch. I looked for Aaron as we left, but saw no sign of him. I worried about it as we piled into Susan's big SUV but my worries faded when we got to the restaurant and the pitcher of margaritas was put down on the table.

I spent a pleasant two hours, forgetting my troubles and worries about Sam, Charlie, the Money, and grades. For a brief time I was just one of the girls, out for a slightly alcoholic lunch, without a care in the world.

My worries came cascading back when we drove back to the school and I saw Aaron sitting in a dark blue sedan by the side entrance, the engine running. "There he is," I said despondently. "Damn, I was hoping he'd be sick or something. I really don't want to go to this funeral."

"You're too kind-hearted for your own good," Barb said with a tequila-laden giggle. "You need to learn to curb that habit."

"Figure you're earning brownie points in heaven," Susan said as she pulled up next to my Jeep so I could drop off my book bag. "Besides, it's just a couple of hours." She peered across the lot, where Aaron was watching us anxiously. "He looks like he needs all the help he can get."

She was right. Even at this distance I could see how worried he looked. Of course his dark suit added to his gloomy appearance. I tossed my gear into the back seat of the Jeep. "Thanks, girls. Stay in touch."

"Will do." "Call me later." "Talk to you."

I waved good-bye as Susan drove to the adjoining row of cars to drop off the next ELL. I hurried toward Aaron, who was driving slowly toward me. "Where have you been?" I asked as I slipped into the passenger seat. "Everybody at school and at work is worried about you." I glanced into the back seat of the car and saw a pile of schoolbooks, strewn around in disarray.

"I've been busy. I've had a lot of things to think about."

"What about school? You missed your tests. That's a biggie, Aaron. You're going to have to talk to Matt and Ed and see if they'll let you make them up." I buckled my seat belt as we pulled away from the curb. "I don't know if you can make up the Woody final. You know you're supposed to identify plants for the test. I don't know if they can reschedule that."

"I'm not worried about it. I've got more important things to worry about."

I examined him. It looked like whatever he was worried about was aging him. His face was thinner and drawn, with deep grooves near his mouth and around his blue but bloodshot eyes. He looked like he aged ten years in a few days. Even his hair looked dry and flyaway, as if all his youth was leached out.

I decided not to quibble with him. "Do you know where this funeral is today?"

He nodded. "It's at a church near the University. It's not far from their house."

"Their?"

"The Peavey family."

"Do you know them well?" I asked as we drove into the outer suburbs of Minneapolis.

His hands slid around the steering wheel in a nervous, stroking gesture. "I've met them."

"Aaron, what's wrong?" I watched as he clenched then unclenched the steering wheel.

"Didn't you get my email?"

I thought guiltily of the email I relegated to my SPAM bucket. "I'm sorry. I didn't get it. What did you send?"

"I sent it again this morning," he said morosely. "When you didn't answer, I resent it. Someone needs to know what's happening."

"I'll check it when I get home," I said soothingly. "Just tell me what's in the message. What's wrong?"

He stared straight ahead, his mouth working as he chewed anxiously on his lower lip. His skin looked smooth and so young looking compared to Sam's tanned, lined face. It was odd. While I recognized Aaron was handsome, he didn't appeal to me. Sam did, with his lined face and small crow wings around his eyes. When did that happen?

When did youth lose its appeal? I decided not to pursue my line of thought. "Aaron? What's wrong?"

He just shook his head and I opted not to press him. We were merging onto the freeway and he needed all his attention to negotiate the heavy traffic and inevitable highway construction.

Ten minutes later we exited the freeway and Aaron drove through the maze of streets around the University of Minnesota. "You know your way around really well," I commented as he took a series of turns on one-way streets to bring us to a residential neighborhood not far from the campus. "I never went to school here so I always get confused and end up lost."

"I grew up not far from here," he said as he maneuvered the car into the crowded parking lot. "It hasn't changed much." We exited the car and joined a queue of people going up the limestone stairs into the small rectangular church.

I took the folded agenda from an usher and followed Aaron into the dark interior. The church was almost full, light streaming into the open nave through the stained glass windows high above. We got seats near the front on the right side and as I sat down, I caught a glimpse of Sam, seated in the center and a row or two behind us. I felt his gaze on us as we took our seats. "Sam's back there," I whispered to Aaron when he slid onto the pew next to me, his long legs pointed toward the aisle. "Sam Barlow?" I prompted when he didn't reply. "Your boss? Our boss?"

He didn't say anything. His attention was on the widow at the front of the church, who sat staring straight ahead. A man was seated next to her but she was angled away from him, ignoring him and focusing on the pulpit, a large metallic urn, and flowers on the small stage-thing at the front. The crowd in front of me shifted position and I had a better view of her.

Sheila Barlow Peavey was as white as a ghost, with two hectic red spots of color on her cheeks. Despite her paleness she was still lovely in a brittle, fragile way, like Jackie O was pretty at her husband's funeral so many years ago. Sheila kept blinking but I saw no telltale hankie in sight. I was surprised the man next to her didn't offer one, but they didn't seem to be together. He was a big, square-faced man, his torso straining his dark suit coat and a thick neck almost disappearing into his shoulders. "Who's the linebacker with the widow?" I asked in a low voice.

Aaron shot me a look of such anger I recoiled, brushing against the old man on my right. "Excuse me," I murmured, dropping my program and bending to get it.

He bent at the same time. "It's the cops," he whispered as our heads almost touched.

"What?" I almost pitched face forward in surprise.

"She was arrested this morning for Mike's murder. They're 'escorting' her today." The old man straightened up and handed me the program.

"Are you sure?" I leaned forward slightly so I could see the widow, who hadn't moved.

"It was on the news," he whispered in return.

"Whoa," I breathed. I turned to tell Aaron this news but he was staring so fixedly at Sheila Peavey I hesitated. He leaned forward, his hands on his thighs and his fingers digging into them as he jiggled his left leg up and down. Sweat stood out in small beads on his forehead and a tiny vein on his right temple bounced in time to his leg. He reminded me of a sports fan who exerted every ounce of concentration on a game in the belief his energy could affect the outcome. I followed his gaze and at that moment Sheila Peavey turned her head slightly.

Their eyes met. Her expression changed. Her face softened and she smiled, just a sad little upturning of her lips. His leg stilled and his fingers relaxed, opening and closing on his thighs as he strained forward.

Suddenly I knew.

Aaron and Sheila Peavey had been—or were still—lovers.

"Holy shit," I whispered. "Aaron, are you and she—"

The man next to Sheila shifted position and she jerked her face back to the front again, her expression impassive and cool. Aaron made a small, choking noise then breathed out a long, hoarse sigh. Music swelled from somewhere behind us as the service began. People around me lurched to their feet and I followed suit mechanically, my brain in a twirl.

I didn't hear a word of the song or the service that followed. Aaron and Sheila, lovers? I tried to remember what I knew about Sheila Peavey. She was younger than Sam. If I remembered right, he went to college after his stint in the Marines, so she was probably ten or fifteen years younger than him. But even so, it still made her at least twenty years older than Aaron.

Twenty years. A world of difference to a teenager. A world of difference to a woman who was facing the future alone and unsure of herself.

I stole a look at him. He still stared at her, his eyes intent and focused only on her. She was a beautiful woman, but...I shook my head, trying to make sense of it. I read about these kinds of things in the papers—Demi Moore and what's-his-name, for example—but I never understood it.

I suddenly remembered one summer when Charlie worked at the country club while he was in college. I overheard him and John laughing about some of the older women there who hit on them. They were embarrassed but also a bit proud of the fact an 'older woman' found them attractive.

I was thoroughly occupied by my chaotic thoughts for the entire ceremony. As the event concluded Sheila Peavey stood and went forward to touch the metallic urn. Then she turned and strode up the aisle near us, the big bulky man one step behind her. Aaron kept his eyes riveted on her as she passed but she didn't pause to look at him or anyone as she left.

Because we were near the front we were among the first ones out of the church. We emerged into late afternoon sunlight, Aaron straining forward in the crowd and almost running out ahead of me. Sheila Peavey was nowhere in sight, but a large dark sedan was pulling away from the curb. I was afraid Aaron would dash off after it and I was just getting ready to grab his arm when a man stepped in front of us. He looked like an older, more careworn version of Aaron.

"Aaron, we have to talk." He gave me a cursory look. "Excuse me. I'm Aaron's father. I need to speak with him."

Aaron looked at me, his eyes bewildered then he docilely nodded as the older man drew him to one side, away from the people coming out of the church.

Suddenly Sam was at my side. Today he wore dark slacks and shirt with a dark gray sports coat. The outfit contrasted beautifully with his salt-and-pepper hair. "Pretty exciting, hmm?" he asked quietly.

"What?"

"Sheila being taken away in custody."

I watched Aaron, his head bent and his face sad as he listened to whatever his father was saying. "I suppose so." I hesitated, wondering if Sam suspected about Aaron and his ex-wife. Probably not. If he did, I don't think Sam would have kept his opinion of Sheila to himself.

Sam glanced at Aaron and his father. "I wonder if Joe will inherit the company because Mike's dead," he mused. "That's often a standard business arrangement."

"Do you think Aaron and your ex-wife...?" I let my voice trail away. What proof did I have? And even if Aaron and Sheila Peavey were lovers, what business was it of anyone? "I don't know," I said lamely, moving out of the way of others who were leaving the church. "I don't know much about business."

"Listen, Cassie." Sam stuck his hands in his pants pockets and stared intently at the ground then looked up at me from under his lashes, his eyes confused. "I'm sorry about last night. I don't know how we got off track. I like you a lot. I think we've got a chance to maybe have something good together. I didn't mean to suggest it wasn't important to me. It is."

Aaron strode past us, making a beeline for his car, ignoring me. "I've got to go, Sam. My ride's leaving." I started after Aaron.

"I can give you a lift." He put a hand on my arm. "We can talk."

Aaron was almost running across the parking lot. "I'd better go with him. We left my car at school and he's supposed to give me a ride back there. Give me a call tonight."

Sam dropped my arm like it was radioactive. "Sure." His voice was cool.

"Damn it, Sam. Aaron's upset about something. I need to go with him." I gave up on an explanation. Aaron was at his car and fumbling with his car keys. "Call me." I hesitated then added, "Please."

I didn't wait to gauge his reaction. I hurried

across the parking lot, dodging other funeral-goers and got to Aaron as he was clicking the door opener. "Hey, leaving without me?" I asked breathlessly.

He looked down at me, his eyes distant and wide. "What?"

"We rode together, remember?" I looked back at Sam, who stared at us. He shook his head and turned away, his face hard and angry. When Aaron's father approached him they shook hands then started to talk, their heads bent close together.

Aaron looked down at the car keys in his hands. "It's not right. They shouldn't have arrested her. It's not right. It's not fair."

"I'm sure the police have a good reason for what they're doing. We can hear about it on the news tonight." Good heavens, if the poor boy was in love with Sheila, what was he feeling now? I could only imagine.

"But it's not right." I saw a tear trickle down his cheek.

"Why don't I drive?" I plucked the keys from his fingers.

He didn't protest but stumbled around to the passenger side of the car. I fiddled with the controls, adjusting everything to my satisfaction then I carefully backed the car out and edged my way out of the crowded lot. I glanced at Aaron. He was staring straight ahead, tears rolling down his face.

"Oh, Aaron." My heart broke to see his sadness. The poor kid, if he was in love with Sheila, how devastating this must be for him. I rooted around in my purse and found a package of tissues. "Here," I said, thrusting them at him.

He took the little package but just held them, staring straight ahead. "Aaron, it's not the end of the world, believe me," I said desperately as I manhandled the unfamiliar sedan through the equally unfamiliar city streets. I tried to recreate our

205

previous route in my head but I hadn't paid attention and soon got turned around, my lack of direction further complicated by globs of college students who occasionally meandered in front of us with the confidence of ignorant youth. I managed to restrain my cursing but just barely.

"I don't mean to be heartless, Aaron, but believe me when I say, this will pass. I know what it feels like, but you'll get over it." I finally saw a sign for the freeway and breathed a sigh of relief.

"I can't get over it," he said in a raw, choked voice. "She confessed because of me. She said she did it. She's trying to protect me."

I merged with the other traffic on a narrow, suicide-inducing onramp. "If she confessed, she probably did it. The police must have evidence, too. They don't just go around and arrest people for the hell of it." I narrowly missed a behemoth SUV piloted by a tiny woman with a cell phone pressed to her ear. "Bitch," I muttered as I got the sedan onto the highway and into the flow of traffic.

"I killed him," he said in a strange, distant voice.

"Say what?" I hazarded a quick glance over my left shoulder, saw an opening, and gunned the sedan into the far left lane, away from other merging traffic ahead. I relaxed slightly. We just had to stay on this road for another few miles then we could take an intersecting highway to the school.

"I killed him."

I shot Aaron a quick look. He was clutching the package of tissues in a death grip as tears flowed down his face. "What?" *It must be shock*, I thought. "What do you mean, Aaron?"

"I killed him. Why are they arresting her?"

Chapter 18

"What are you talking about?" I looked at him then I glanced in the rear view mirror. A big black pickup truck was on our car's tail, the driver glaring impatiently at me. I looked at our speedometer and realized I had let the speed slack off. I gave the car some gas and clutched the wheel, praying for a clear head. "What?"

"I stabbed him." Aaron stared out his window now, tears still flowing down his face. "It solved so many problems. My father would keep his job and Sheila and I could be together. It just made so much sense."

I opened, closed, then opened my mouth again. "Aaron, you're wrong. You didn't kill him. He was poisoned. That's what Sam said, at least."

He didn't seem to hear me. He stared straight ahead, his handsome face twisted with grief and fear. His mouth was clenched so tightly in a frown it was painful just to see. "When I went out to look for him at the dedication ceremony, I found him alone in the greenhouse. I stabbed him. You saw the blood. I killed him. Sheila said she poisoned him to save me."

What about evidence? What about blood tests

and tox tests and crime scene investigation? I kept those thoughts to myself. "Where did you put the knife?"

"It was just a pocket knife. It didn't take much. He was leaning on one of the benches. He looked sick. When he saw me coming he asked me to help."

I glanced at Aaron and saw the haunted look on his face. "What happened?" I whispered.

"I stabbed him. It was easy. He wasn't expecting it. He fell down right away." Aaron took a deep, shuddering breath. "I put the knife in my pocket and walked out with it. I threw it in the river that night." He laughed bitterly. "No one suspected me."

He was right. I had focused on the obvious signs of poison and I suspect the authorities did, too. Both Aaron and I were questioned but it was perfunctory. As far as anyone knew, none of us had any connection to Michael Peavey.

I was suddenly dizzy, my brain in shock but I forced myself to think. A tricky bit of freeway was just ahead where two other freeways merged with this one. I kept the car in the left lane, away from the mergers and said, "None of that matters, Aaron. Sheila did it. She poisoned him. You have to accept it."

He shook his head adamantly. "You don't understand. There's nothing for me if I don't have Sheila."

The stress building in me for days started to bubble to the surface. Charlie, Sam, school, the inheritance, Kathleen, the Pervert, a new house—all flashed through my mind in a little kaleidoscope of images until my head buzzed with memory. "Look, Aaron." I tried to keep my voice reasonable, but I wasn't sure I succeeded. "I'm twice your age. Hell, more than twice. Believe me when I say that you have a lot of living to do in the next few decades. You'll look back on this and be stunned by how terrible you thought it all was." Then I reconsidered. "Okay, yes, it is terrible. You thought you killed a man and you thought someone loved you, but believe me it's not the end of the world. It's not as bad as you think."

"I love her," he said, his voice raw with longing. "She's everything to me."

I took a deep breath, pushing my own anger and resentment as far from my voice as I could. "I remember being your age, I remember what it's like to be twenty years old and love someone so much it hurts. Charlie and I were in love then. He was handsome and sweet and kind and my heart just about broke with loving him."

"So why are you divorced?"

The harsh words made me blink in surprise. "What?"

"If you loved him so much, why are you divorced? Why didn't it work?"

I gaped at him like a waterless fish. I had no good answer. Luckily I had to deal with traffic, which gave me the time I needed to come up with a reasonably coherent answer. "We just weren't right for each other," I finally managed.

"I don't believe that. How could somebody be so handsome and loving and kind and not be right for you?"

I thought fleetingly of Sam, with his prickly exterior and his sad, lonely face. Then I thought of Charlie, whose suave exterior also hid sadness. "I don't know," I said honestly. "But it just didn't work out for Charlie and me."

"Are you saying it won't work out for Sheila and me? Is it the age difference?"

"She killed her husband, Aaron!" I longed to shake him but I had my hands full with six lanes of traffic, construction ahead, and a monster truck on my car's butt. "It's got nothing to do with age."

"I know what must have happened." He sounded like he was thinking out loud. "We met the other night and I told her I did it. She was so surprised."

Of course she was, I thought. *She thought she murdered her husband and this poor besotted kid steps up and says he did it. What a gift.* I was surprised the police hadn't arrested him yet. What was she waiting for? Why hadn't she turned him in? I tried to chide myself for such an uncharitable thought, but I remembered Sheila Peavey's peremptory manner when she confronted Sam at the store. She was a woman who was accustomed to getting her way. She would have no qualms about using Aaron if it suited her needs.

"We didn't have enough time to talk. I called her later but she said she couldn't talk to me so we couldn't discuss what to do. I should have tried to see her. She's doing this to protect me. I know she is."

I closed my eyes as though I could block out the feeling his words evoked. The naked longing and fear came from the little boy still inside him but the words themselves were adult words. I was sharply reminded this was a young man—and the key word was *young.* I stared at the darkening spring sky, struggling desperately to truly remember what it felt like to be so young and so in love.

"We don't know exactly what's going on," I said, picking my words with care. "The best thing we can do right now is contact the police and talk to them." I gripped the wheel so hard my hands started to cramp. I relaxed my fingers but the tension just moved to my back where tired muscles began to tighten. I glanced behind us and the monster truck was still there, a metal dragon breathing fire down my backside. I sped up until I could safely move into the center lane. As soon as I did, the pickup breezed by us going at least ninety. I muttered a curse in his direction and starting angling our car toward the right lane and our upcoming exit. "You didn't kill him, Aaron. Sheila did."

He shook his head. "I stabbed him. He fell down."

"He was already sick."

"I killed him and now she's going to prison. What will I do without her?"

I longed to howl *You'll get on with your life! You're twenty years old and you've got a lot of living yet to do! Don't waste your life like this!* "We can talk to the police," I said, babbling anything I could to keep the conversation rolling. "I'm sure we can find some kind of mitigating circumstance. You can't take the fall for this. She killed him, Aaron."

"No!"

His voice startled me so much I jerked the wheel and our tires rattled over the sleep-strip on the shoulder. I tugged the wheel again and we were back on smooth pavement. "Shit, Aaron, don't do that, I'm driving." I considered the exit coming up fast on our right. It was two exits before the one we needed for school. Maybe I should get off and find a police station. As soon as I considered it, I dismissed the idea. I had no idea where anything was on this side of town. How could I hope to find a police station?

I returned to my original plan: get us to school and maybe I could find one of the instructors or somebody else to help. I increased our speed slightly as though I could magically make the next three miles disappear. "Don't talk to the police unless you have a lawyer," I said. "I'll call Charlie. He might know somebody who can help. He doesn't handle criminal law but I'll bet he knows somebody who does."

"I don't need a lawyer. I'm going to confess and be done with it."

"Don't do anything rash." I shifted lanes, moving

past the law-abiding slow pokes in the right lane and merging with the speedier demons in the center lane. "Don't make any statements to the police and don't admit to anything. If you're lucky, they'll take your youth into account."

"I don't want them to, don't you understand?"

"No, I don't," I snapped, my patience finally at the breaking point. "You're throwing your life away, and for what?" When he didn't answer, I glanced at him. He was staring at me as though I was the stupidest idiot on the planet. "Well?"

"Love."

I longed to beat my head against the steering wheel, but I didn't dare. "This isn't some damn book," I said through clenched teeth. "Life doesn't work that way, Aaron. Don't sacrifice yourself for love. You're too young to waste yourself."

"You don't know anything about it."

The quiet conviction in his voice brought tears to my eyes. All the pain I felt so long ago when Charlie and I broke up washed back over me, the old memories so strong I was nauseous with them. Why didn't those memories die? Why did they keep coming back to haunt me? I took a long, steadying breath. "Of course I do. I've been in love."

"But you got divorced."

"That's not the point, Aaron. I've been in love."

"I know you've loved. But did you ever fall in love again after the first time?"

The question startled me. "What? Of course I did."

"Did you? Did you have the same kind of love? Did you ever love anybody the same way again? Or did you lose that when you got divorced?"

I couldn't reply because I couldn't lie. I never loved anyone the way I loved Charlie. But was that so terrible? Was there a difference between 'in love' and 'loving?' Of course there was, but this wasn't the time to get into metaphysical discussions about the nature of love. "This isn't about me, it's about you."

He laughed bitterly. "Look where you are now. You're divorced and alone."

"Now just a minute. There are worse things than being divorced and alone!"

"Like what?"

"Like being in a loveless marriage. Like not being happy with the person you're married to. Like living a lie."

"That's what Sheila was doing." His voice was a low whisper, full of sadness. "Living a lie. She said when she was with me, she was real again."

I had no answer, no rebuttal. How could I talk to a child so in love he was willing to throw his life away? "Don't do anything rash," I repeated. "Just wait and talk to your father or to a lawyer." I spied our exit ahead and breathed a sigh of relief. I darted around a slow poke in a big Benz sedan and got into the right lane, prepared to exit and end this nightmarish trip. Only another mile and we'd be back at the school. How could I get someone out to the parking lot to help me? My cell phone was buried in my purse somewhere plus it was almost four-thirty and most people would be leaving the school for the day. Maybe instead of campus I should drive to the nearby town? It was only a few blocks away, but I had the same problem there I'd had at the earlier exit. I had no idea where a police station was located.

I slowed our breakneck pace and took the exit at sixty, entering the county highway with the school just ahead. "Park the car," Aaron said as the campus came into sight. "I have to go inside for a minute."

"What for?" I turned into the west entrance road. As I suspected the parking lot was almost empty. The day students were all gone home and the night students weren't there yet. It was the witching

213

hour at school.

"I need to clean out my locker."

"It can wait. You have to talk to your father and get a lawyer." I pulled up next to my Jeep, now parked alone with the nearest car two rows away. A light mist began to fall, replacing the earlier spring sunlight. It matched my mood, which was pissed off, nervous, and foggy-minded.

As soon as I slowed the car, Aaron jumped out. "Hey!" I jammed the gear into park, taking up at least three parking spaces, and jerked the keys out of the ignition. He was dashing toward the building as though demons were chasing him. Who knows? Maybe they were.

I started to follow then realized I needed to call the police. I plopped my purse on the hood of the car and plunged my hand in, miraculously coming up with my cell phone after only a second or two of groping. I opened it and dialed 9-1-1 as I hurried toward the building. When the operator came on the line, I simply said there was a distraught young man at the school who needed help. I didn't want to get into a detailed explanation and besides, Aaron wasn't going to harm anyone. If anything I needed to be worried he might harm himself.

The thought made me stop in my tracks just as Ed came out of the building, papers under one arm and a travel thermos in his hand. "Hey there," he called out with a big grin. "What are you doing back here? You're done with school."

"Aaron," I muttered. "Where did he go?"

"I just passed him," Ed said, craning his neck to look back into the building. "He was running down the hall. I thought he was out sick. He's missed all his tests. I was talking with the other instructors about it."

I rushed past him, heading for the door. As I did, a dark maroon SUV pulled in front of me, blocking my way. I was almost hit by the driver's door as Sam swung it open. "Where is he?" he demanded, jumping out.

I didn't stop to wonder how he knew. "Inside. Come on." The man from the funeral—Aaron's father—jumped out of the passenger side and slammed the door behind him.

"This way," I said, grabbing the heavy glass door to the building and flinging it open.

"What's going on, Cassie?" I heard Ed's voice fade behind us as I raced into the building.

"How did you know?" I asked Sam over my shoulder as I led the way down the hallway to the Horticulture classrooms. The transition from the brighter outdoors to the gloomy hallway made me pause momentarily then I got my bearings and barreled ahead.

"Joe was worried," Sam said, easily keeping up with me on my right side. "This is Joe Swenson, Aaron's dad." He gestured to the man on my left side.

I glanced at him. He nodded once then focused on the end of the hallway where a door stood ajar.

"Cassie, what's going on?" Ed called out behind us.

"I'm worried about Aaron." I took a right turn at the hallway intersection and we emerged into the Horticulture wing of the building. The lights were dimmer here with every other overhead light lit. I could see down the length of the hall and no one was standing by the lockers. "He said he was going to his locker." I hurried around a half-corner and burst into the potting room that served as foyer to the new greenhouse that we had inaugurated just a few days before.

The big room was empty and the double doors to the greenhouse were locked. I peered through the glass side windows but saw no movement inside.

"Where is he?" I looked around, but there was nowhere he could be unless...I raced to the pesticide locker and jerked on the door but it was locked securely.

"What is it?" Ed asked, pushing through the door. "Sam, what are you doing here?"

"Aaron Swenson," Joe Swenson said urgently. "Where did he go?"

Ed shrugged. "I didn't see. The classrooms are locked and the only thing open is the old greenhouse. Matt was going to come back later and lock it up, too. I thought Aaron was—"

I didn't wait for him to finish. I dashed out of the room and back down the hallway, heading for the main door to the greenhouse, the door where I saw Sam exit a week earlier. I grabbed the handle but it didn't move.

"Damn. It's locked." I pounded on the door, but it was solid metal and didn't budge no matter how hard I beat on it.

"Aaron! Come out, son!" his father shouted. "Come out, we can talk about this."

"Talk about what?" Ed asked, looking in confusion from me to Sam then to Joe, who now pounded on the door.

"Aaron's upset about something," I said, pushing past Ed in the tight confines of the hall outside the main door. "I'm worried about him."

Ed stared at me for a brief second then he dropped the papers he was carrying, letting them land in a whoosh of dust on the floor. He put his travel mug on top. "Come on. Let's use the back way." We raced each other down the hallway to the rear exit I used a week earlier when I heard the two men arguing in the greenhouse. "It shouldn't be locked," Ed said as he reached for the door handle and pulled.

It didn't budge.

"Damn!" I looked with despair at Sam, who followed us. "He's in there."

Ed pulled a ring of keys from the retractable loop at his belt and quickly sorted through them. "Let me try this..." He inserted the key in the lock and it turned, but the door still didn't budge. "It's bolted on the inside," he muttered. "Somebody must have set the fire door."

I almost groaned out loud. The two doors from the greenhouse leading into the main school building had fire doors that could be closed in case of a pesticide spill, fire, or other dangerous problem. The doors served as a barrier to the rest of the world, effectively isolating anyone in the greenhouse unless they used the emergency exit.

Ed and I exchanged a desperate look then he turned and headed back the way we came. "There are no exterior exits except for the emergency door. We can go outside and look in. Maybe he's not in there. Maybe Matt locked the greenhouse."

Sam looked at me and I shook my head. "He's in there," I whispered. I followed Ed to the potting room and the door near the pesticide locker. It led behind the building and was used primarily to schlep tools in when we were too lazy to use the service entrance fifty yards away. Ed pushed open the door and led the way to the left, around the exterior of the new greenhouse and past a collection of wheelbarrows and wooden pallets stored against the north side of the school. The old greenhouse was set into a recess in the building, the walls and glass fogged now in the late afternoon sunlight and the condensation that formed throughout the day.

"That's odd," Ed said as we neared the west wall of the greenhouse.

"Don't you have it regulated?" Sam demanded, staring at the moist panes of glass.

"Have what regulated?" I stared dumbly at the

greenhouse then at Sam.

"It shouldn't be so damp," he said, pressing his face against the glass and peering inside. "The windows should have opened to allow ventilation."

I struggled to remember my basic nursery ops facts. The old greenhouse was a relic from another age but we did have a rudimentary ventilation system that was supposed to open when the humidity got too high or if it was too warm in the house. Excess moisture and heat were prime breeders of mold and we battled it often in the wintertime when the bright winter sun heated the space until the glass walls dripped condensation.

"We do have a system," I said. "I monitored it last week when I saw you and Michael Peavey. It's part of our duties."

"Whose duties?"

"Nursery ops students," Ed said, passing us and going to the east side of the greenhouse. "It's wet here, too. It shouldn't be." He ducked, peering into the greenhouse. "It's not moisture. It's something else."

Sam sniffed the cool spring air. "What kind of gas do you use? When was the last time the house was fumigated?"

"None of the students have access to those gases," Ed said. "We keep the fumigants locked because none of the students are certified to use them." He touched the keys dangling from his belt. "They're locked. I'm sure of it."

"Fumiga..." I looked around desperately and spied some lumber in a discarded pile near the pallets. I grabbed a board almost as tall as me and aimed toward the lower panes of glass, using it like a jousting lance.

Sam was faster. He bent down and picked up a football-sized rock that was part of the edging material near the low concrete wall of the greenhouse. "Where's the emergency door?" he asked, hefting the rock.

"Over here." I tucked my makeshift battering ran under my arm, running awkwardly past Ed to point to the metal door set into the wall where the glass intersected the building. Sam stood back and threw the rock at the lower pane of glass near the door's handle. It cracked the thick pane of glass but didn't break it. These structures were built to withstand hail and wind, so I wasn't surprised.

He didn't pause but picked up the rock again, using both arms to throw it at the crack he made. This succeeded in widening the crack and putting a dent in the surface of the glass.

Ed picked up the board I had dropped and swung it like a bat. The crack widened and a small hole appeared in the middle. He swung again and the glass finally shattered, a cloud of noxious fumes billowing outward.

"Aaron!" I shouted, moving toward the hole.

"Get back!" Sam jerked me so roughly I almost fell. "Stay back!"

"But he might be—" I peered past Sam and saw the cloud thinning as it met the outside air. I ducked, trying to see under it. "Can you see him? Is he in there?" I asked Ed, who moved away and peered inside through a glass pane two feet away from the gaping hole.

"I can't tell. I think..." He moved back, his face ashen. "He's in there."

"Joe, no!" Sam released me and grabbed Aaron's father, who was rushing forward. "Joe, don't, it's dangerous!"

I heard sirens in the distance. I knew they'd be too late.

Chapter 19

"I couldn't convince him," I said tiredly as I slumped on a chair in a classroom and buried my face in my hands. "I tried to convince him it would be okay but he didn't want to hear. Oh, God. He was so young. This shouldn't have happened."

"It's not your fault, Cassie." Sam sat near me, his desk chair pulled close to mine so he could put an arm around my shoulders. "You did what you could. He was desperately in love." His voice was so low I almost didn't hear him but I felt the grief and anguish in it. "Damn her. I know what kind of..." He took a long shuddering breath and I looked up at him enquiringly.

"What kind of what?" I asked softly.

Sam closed his eyes briefly but not before I saw memories of old grief replace the new grief there. "Sheila was a remarkable woman." I tried to decipher that little cryptic clue. He must have seen my puzzlement. He leaned closer. "She had a way of making a man feel like he was the greatest gift to women and it wasn't just the sex. Later, when I was alone, I knew I was being manipulated, but by then it was too late. I can't imagine a young kid, somebody who..." He hesitated, looking for words, "...somebody whose ego wasn't solid yet. Poor kid."

"I can't believe he did it," I whispered. "Good Lord, he ruined his life for her. What makes a person do something like that?" I looked at Sam. "You must know how it felt. You created a plant for your wife. I've never done anything like that for someone I loved."

He looked at me oddly. "I didn't create a plant for her."

"Sheila's Sunrise. You told me about it."

"I didn't name it," he said. "It was unnamed when I created it. Mike must have named it." He smiled wryly. "I didn't love Sheila that much." His gaze went to the doorway and the emergency personnel we could hear in the hall. "I didn't love her that much," he repeated.

Tears rolled down my face as I thought of Aaron, now lying dead on the floor in the greenhouse in almost exactly the same spot where Michael Peavey died a week earlier. I didn't see Aaron's body, but I heard the emergency workers talking about what they found. Aaron learned his school lessons well. When heated, malathion emitted toxic fumes. I vaguely remember the particular class when Ed discussed its use and how inadvertent exposure to heating resulted in deadly fumes. The effects were gruesome.

Aaron was no longer one of the handsomest boys I'd ever known.

Poor Aaron must have remembered those lessons, too. "Where did he get the chemicals?" I asked brokenly, forcing the words out around a sob.

"The pesticide locker was still intact," Ed said from across the room. He sat at the teacher's desk, his face ashen. He had donned a HazMat suit and gone into the greenhouse, helping the professional HazMat team negotiate the narrow aisles between the potting benches. I'm sure he got a good look at Aaron's body before it was removed. He looked stunned and his hand trembled when he lifted his travel mug of coffee to take a sip.

"All he had to do was sneak some out of the locker when it was unlocked," I said, taking the box of tissues Sam handed me. "It was unlocked now and again. If he was planning this for a while or if he thought he might need it..."

Ed shook his head. "I can't believe it. He had so much going for him. What was it? Why would he do it?"

I heard a voice I recognized among the babble of voices in the hallway outside the classroom. A second later Charlie walked into the room. "Cassie, are you okay?" he asked, striding to me. I leapt to my feet and he took me in his arms, holding me tightly against him.

I buried my face in his suit coat. "How did you know?" I asked, my voice muffled.

"Mary Hannon called me."

I looked up at Charlie then at Sam, who watched us from his seat. His face was calm and still, but I saw the hurt in his dark eyes. "You called her?" I asked.

"I told her to call him," Sam said, his glance flicking to Charlie then back to me. "I figured you could use the..." He shrugged. "Whatever."

"Thank you," I whispered.

"You're okay?" Charlie demanded, pulling away to look down at me. He smoothed my hair back from my face, his fingers lingering on my chin. "You're sure?"

I nodded and wiped my nose with the wadded tissue I still clutched. "It was Aaron," I whispered. "He said he stabbed Michael Peavey. But that didn't kill Peavey. The poison did, right?" I looked at Sam for confirmation.

"I don't know the details, but..." Sam lowered his voice, glancing at the doorway where the police personnel were standing. "Amanita mushrooms."

Ed screwed up his face. "Nasty."

"Ooh." I breathed out a long exhalation of breath.

"Is that bad?" Charlie asked, looking at each of us in turn.

For an instant the professor replaced the shocked bystander and Ed said, "Toxic in all forms. No known antidote. Liver failure, toxic shock, total systemic breakdown." Then he looked ashamed, realizing he was dispassionately describing a man's death. "They're not called 'death caps' for nothing. Where did she find them?"

"Walk out into any of the woods around here," Sam said. "Don't forget, Sheila was a trained botanist. She would recognize them."

Ed nodded. "You're right. I've seen them in the windbreak behind the school. They're just emerging now. It would only take one."

"Why didn't he recognize them, though?" I asked, disentangling myself from Charlie and resuming my seat near Sam. "Peavey was a botanist, too, right?" I longed to touch Sam's arm, to try to recapture the closeness we had, but I was sharply aware of Charlie, who moved near to me. I sat still, not sure which way to move lest I touch either man.

Sam shook his head. "Not really. Mike was a research botanist. And he wasn't expecting it. All she had to do is chop them up fine and put them in his food. He'd never know."

"But she must have known the police would trace it back to her." I looked up at Charlie. "Wouldn't they? Surely she would know she'd be a suspect."

Joe Swenson walked into the room, escorted by a uniformed policeman. Sam and I got to our feet. "I'm so sorry," I said hesitantly. "I'm sorry..." It sounded trivial to say 'sorry for your loss' but I didn't know what else would suffice.

Sam brushed by me and went to Swenson. "Are you okay, Joe?"

Swenson sat down abruptly, almost tipping the chair-desk. The policeman took up position near the door, not quite a guard, not quite an eavesdropper.

"I don't know," he said, his voice hoarse and so choked I barely understood the words. "Why did he do it? I don't understand. I knew Sheila was flirting with him, but I had no idea it went so far."

"You knew?" I asked.

"I suspected," he amended. "We argued about it at the funeral today. I wish now..." He closed his eyes and my heart twisted at the sight of such naked grief. "Why didn't I listen to him? Why didn't I try to help?"

Sam's eyes met mine. "You're not to blame," he murmured, his hand on Swenson's shoulder, squeezing gently. "No one's to blame."

"Sheila Peavey is," Swenson rasped out, his voice hate-filled. "That bitch is saying Aaron gave her the mushrooms that killed her husband."

"She said what?" I chopped off the words I wanted to say when Charlie's arm tightened on my shoulder. "That witch," I whispered. If the police believed her, she'd get off scot-free. Aaron would be blamed for the poison and for stabbing Michael Peavey. "Can she get away with it?"

Charlie's arm tightened again. "Are we free to go?" he asked the police officer. "I'm sure Mr. Swenson would like to leave, as well as these others." He nodded toward Ed and me, his gaze sweeping over Sam then returning to the cop at the doorway.

The officer nodded, his face impassive until he looked at Joe Swenson, who stared at the floor, a shocked look on his face. The policeman said softly, "You're free to leave." His gaze moved to me. "You have to go to the station to sign your deposition."

I nodded and Charlie said immediately, "I'll go with you." He shifted slightly so he was facing Joe Swenson. "Will you be okay?" he asked gently.

Sam shot Charlie an impatient look as though to say, *Idiot, of course he won't be.* I had to agree with Sam, it was a stupid question. "I'll go with you, Joe," Sam said, putting a hand under Swenson's arm and helping him to his feet. "We'll talk to your wife together."

Swenson swayed, his eyes unfocused and his face slack with shock. "How am I going to tell her?" he murmured. "Aaron was her joy. How can I tell our daughter?"

Sam put an arm around the man's shoulder. "I'll drive you home. We'll handle it together."

I swiped at the tears dribbling down my cheeks. "Can I help, Sam?" I whispered. "Can I do anything?"

He looked back at me then at Charlie next to me. "Call Mary and tell her what happened. She'll have to tell the other employees." He hesitated then said, "I'll call you later, Cassie. We need to..." His gaze went to Charlie. "We'll talk."

I watched as he and Swenson left, tears rolling down my face.

****

The next afternoon I pulled into the parking lot of Barlow's Nursery and stared at the front door of the storefront. Charlie's Jag was parked in the slot next to mine and I knew he was inside, talking with Mary and Sam about the contract dispute with Sheila Peavey. He called me the night before to check when I was working so he could time his visit with my arrival.

Charlie and I had gone to the local police station

where I repeated as much as I could remember of Aaron's rambling, disjointed conversation in the car on our hectic drive from the funeral. Charlie drove me back to the school then we parted in the parking lot and I drove home on autopilot, nauseous and so shaken it took me two tries to get the Jeep into my garage without knocking off the side mirror.

I spent most of the evening crying and listening to the news, where Aaron's death was discussed *ad nauseum* amid much speculation about his involvement with Michael Peavey. Sheila Peavey was still in custody but not charged. I wondered if she would escape punishment.

I stared at the door leading in to Barlow's and knew it would never be the same for me. I could never resume my duties here without remembering Aaron. I wasn't sure if I could work in the landscape trade again without thinking of him and what he did.

I pushed the gloomy thought aside and went into the building, bypassing the front checkout counters where Bev chatted quietly with a customer. We smiled sadly at each other and I went to the back room where I swapped my purse and car coat for the work coat in my locker. As I closed it I looked at Aaron's locker. Were the condoms still inside? I smiled bitterly at my own naïveté at trying to help him with his 'girlfriend.'

As I started for the back door Charlie emerged from the tiny office, talking with Mary Hannon. I paused to wait for him. The strong spring sunlight coming through the skylight seemed to glow like a halo around him, illuminating the smooth planes of his face and his surprising green eyes. When he smiled at me, I saw the little crinkles at the corner of his eyes and the way his eyes seemed to light with love.

My heart twisted as I remembered Aaron's

distraught words. He was right. I never loved anyone again the way I loved Charlie and I don't think I ever could. That love belonged to the person I was then, the person I left behind in my youth. Was that why I still clung to Charlie? Was it why I still loved him so much?

As he walked across the room to me, I found a partial answer. Yes, I loved him because of my youth but I also loved him because of who he was. Charlie was, quite simply, one of the most loveable men I've ever known. It was easy to love Charlie.

"Going to work?" he asked, watching me slap my gloves against one leg.

"I'm going to try," I said. "But I don't know..." I looked around the big room then to the door leading to the greenhouses. "I don't know." I glanced at Mary, who joined Bev at the checkout counter to chat with the customer. "How did it work out?"

"Because Sheila Peavey's status is uncertain, we can't sign any papers. She and Peavey had no children so if her property becomes forfeit for any reason, we'll deal with her cousin. But for now, it's in limbo."

"So Barlow's will be okay as long as they stay in business?"

"They should be fine if they continue to do well." Behind him I glimpsed Sam leave the office, pausing momentarily when he saw Charlie and me talking. Then he hurried through the building and out the front door. I hated to admit it, but I felt relief at seeing him leave. I wasn't ready to face more emotional roller coasters.

"You could invest in the business, you know," Charlie said.

My attention snapped back to him. "What?" He nodded. "I didn't think of that." I smiled wryly. "I keep forgetting I have money."

"Janelle will remind you." His voice was

laughing and warm when he said her name and I thought, *Aha, there is something still there.* Then he said, "She's a lawyer, after all. We're good at keeping our clients on track."

"Yeah, you are." I swatted my leg again with the gloves. "I have to go, Charlie."

"Mary was wondering if you could look at the computer program again," he said. "She asked me to tell you. They have some more things to add to it."

"Sure." *Anything to postpone going into the greenhouse,* I thought. I started toward the office and Charlie hesitated. "Are you leaving?" I asked.

"Soon. I thought I'd walk around, look the place over." He smiled but it didn't quite reach his eyes. "I may want to invest, too."

I raised one eyebrow. "You? Invest in a landscape company?"

He shrugged. "You never know. Cassie..."

"Hmm?"

Charlie's eyes met and held mine with an intensity I hadn't seen in a long time. "I'm sorry about all the crap going on. I love you. I want you to be happy." I was surprised and he must have seen it. "All this stuff that's been happening. It's made me think." He kissed me quickly on the cheek. "Be happy." He looked like he wanted to say something more but instead he turned and headed for Mary, who turned to greet him with a smile. That wasn't unusual. Everybody smiled when they saw Charlie.

I stared after him for a long minute, not sure what I just heard. Then I went into the office. The computer was on. I sat down and logged in, bringing up the computer program I'd been working on. As the desktop materialized in front of me, I saw an email icon in the corner and suddenly realized I hadn't checked email in the last day. Aaron said he sent me something. I thought about it for a couple of seconds then opened a web browser to access my personal email.

I had a few emails from the more techno-savvy ELLs, demanding to know what happened. I shunted those aside to deal with later. I opened my SPAM bucket and skimmed through the assorted enticements to 'enlarge my male pleasure principal' and 'refinance now at astronomically low rates.' About halfway through the queue I saw it, buried among the 'schlongDikMegaMan' ads. I clicked open the email and leaned forward to read.

Gidget: I don't know who else to talk to. You always listened to me. Maybe you'll listen now. Nobody else will believe me.

Sheila and I were out walking one day and we saw the mushrooms and she laughed and said something like, oh, I know what I can do with that. I told her they were poisonous and she said she knew.

She's wrong, though. I killed him. I saw him in the greenhouse and I stabbed him. I wanted you to know. I want somebody to know how much I loved her and why I killed him. I don't want you to think I'm some stupid kid who doesn't know the consequences of what he's doing. I do know. I did it because I loved her. I tried to put Barlow's out of business so she could sell the land. I killed her husband so my father could keep his job and so I could be with her. I'm not a stupid kid. I want to be with her and I know what might happen to me. I want that happy life everybody talks about and no one gets. I'm going to do it no matter what the cost.

Aaron

Why did he send this to me? I checked the timestamp and knowledge flooded through me. He sent it yesterday morning. The morning of the funeral. He was planning to confess. He knew it was all coming apart and he didn't want Sheila to go to jail. "Oh, Aaron," I murmured, touching the words on the screen. The greenhouse, the fumigant, his death...he planned it all along. It wasn't spontaneous, the way I thought.

I carefully saved the email into a file and printed it then I stored a copy on the hard drive and moved the original email into a special electronic folder. I would need to see the police as soon as possible and give them this. Maybe it was enough to bring charges against Sheila Peavey. I wasn't sure any more about anything. I'd leave it to the authorities to figure out.

I folded the printout and put it into my back pocket then skimmed through the rest of the email queue in case Aaron sent something else. Despite the grim message I just read, I had to smile at some of the subject lines I saw. "Is your penis size too small? I can change it." I shook my head in disbelief.

"I know you can change it," a husky voice said behind me. "Get naked and I'll show you." I spun the chair in a dizzying circle. Sam leaned against the doorframe, his arms crossed against his chest. He smiled at me and came into the room. "Care to try it?" His tone was light but I heard an undercurrent of insecurity in his words. This wasn't some teasing, silly question. He was truly asking...what?

I stood up, my knees shaking. I met him halfway across the office, not pausing until he was just an inch or so away from me. I wrapped my arms around his neck. "Yes," I said. "I think I'd like to try it."

His kiss was sweet and welcoming with that undercurrent of passion I'd come to expect from him, that sense of 'man' held in reserve. Our bodies melded together, his warmth infusing me and my breasts pressing against his hard chest. When we finally broke apart, I leaned back in his arms and he stared down at me. "Are you sure?"

"No," I said honestly. "But it's worth trying." I saw the disappointment in his eyes but he hid it well. "I can't promise anything," I warned. "I've loved

Charlie too long to change now. But I think there might be room for expansion in my life."

Sam smiled slowly. "I can work with a comment like that." He kissed my nose then released me. "Now back to work, you slacker." But his hand lingered on my butt.

I wiggled it against him. "Yes, sir." I picked up my gloves from the desk where I had dropped them. "I don't know how much longer I'll be here," I said as we left the office. I looked around the open store space. "It's too much, I think."

He nodded in understanding. "Take your time. We'll talk about it." Then he winked. "And maybe do more than talk."

"Sam? Can you come here for a minute?" Mary waved to her brother, asking him to join her and Charlie near the checkout counter.

"See you tonight?" Sam murmured.

I nodded. "I'll cook dinner."

"I can take you out," he said.

I grinned. "Maybe we'll get take out and eat it at home."

He looked at me, his dark brown eyes warm and loving. "Thanks, Cassie." He seemed to be trying to decide what to say, finally saying in a rush, "I'll do my best."

"That's all I can ask, Sam." I nodded toward Mary. "The boss calls."

He laughed and walked across the room. What a contrast he was to Charlie. There was Sam in his worn jeans and old flannel shirt and T-shirt, muscles hard and evident under the faded fabric. His white hair was flyaway around his head and his tanned skin looked rough, like a man who perpetually worked outside.

And there was Charlie with his elegant tailored suit, his dark hair without a strand out of place, his smooth face so classically handsome. He looked like

231

a sleek, dark thoroughbred next to Sam's shaggy, sturdy quarter-horse.

Summer/winter. Day/night. Both men turned and looked at me, Charlie's face puzzled but loving and Sam, as usual, impassive and grim until our eyes met. Then he seemed to melt, his face softening as he smiled slowly, impishly.

I love summer with its warm lazy days of swimming at the beach, casual picnics and long walks on the trails followed by an indolent nap in the sun.

I love winter with its frozen afternoons of snowshoeing, hot cocoa at the skating rink, and pristine, clear days of sharp air that made the breath in your lungs feel supercharged.

I smiled at Charlie and Sam and went to join them. I wasn't quite ready to move on to summer yet. I looped my arm through Sam's and leaned against him.

I still had some winter to explore. I was looking forward to it.

A word about the author...

J L Wilson is a Midwestern author who writes "mysteries with a touch of romance...and romance with a touch of gray."

She can be found on Twitter, Facebook, MySpace, and a few blogs here and there.

This link tells you where:
http://tinyurl.com/ak8hl8

Thank you for purchasing
this Wild Rose Press publication.
For other wonderful stories of romance,
please visit our on-line bookstore at
www.thewildrosepress.com.

For questions or more information
contact us at
info@thewildrosepress.com.

The Wild Rose Press
www.TheWildRosePress.com